LIGHT DESCENDING

Books by Kathryn Elizabeth Jones

A River of Stones

Parable Series

> Conquering Your Goliaths: A Parable of the Five Stones
>
> Conquering Your Goliaths: Guidebook
>
> The Feast: A Parable of the Ring
>
> The Gift: A Parable of the Key
>
> The Parables of Virginia Bean

Heaven 24/7 - Living in the Light

Marketing Your Book on a Budget

Susan Cramer Mysteries

> Scrambled
>
> Sunny Side-Up
>
> Hard Boiled
>
> Over Easy

Brianne James Mysteries

> Tie Died
>
> Buckled Inn
>
> Slipped Up – Coming 2020

Mooseberry Mooseberry Goosebery Pie

The Space Adventures of Aaden Prescott

> Light*Shade*
>
> Light*Descending*
>
> Light*Source* – Coming Fall 2020

Enlightened: My Personal Journey with Christ Through Scripture Journaling

The Human Bean

LIGHT DESCENDING

The Space Adventures of Aaden Prescott
Book 2

KATHRYN ELIZABETH JONES

Idea Creations Press
www.ideacreationspress.com

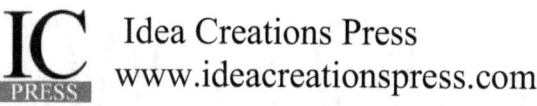

Idea Creations Press
www.ideacreationspress.com

978-1948804172

Publisher's Catalog-In-Publishing Data

Jones, Kathryn Elizabeth, author
Light Descending / Kathryn Elizabeth Jones
First trade paperback original edition. | Salt Lake City: Idea Creations Press, 2020.
ISBN 978-1948804172 | LCCN 2020931741
Science Fantasy | Teen-Fiction. | BISAC: YOUNG ADULT
FICTION / Science Fiction / Alien Contact

Printed in the U. S. A

"Give Light, and the darkness will disappear of itself."

Desiderius Erasmus

After the destruction of Earth, Aaden escapes to the skies, looking for a place to live. Though humanoid, Aaden is not from Earth, and an uncalculated sacrifice must now be made by his family and friends – a sacrifice that will ultimately leave one of them behind.

Journey

Don't laugh. It's amazing what you can forget when you're about to be destroyed. All you can think about is your safety. Later, you realize you're hungry and need a decent bed to sleep in. It's like the last time your mom yelled at you to get in the car – hovercar or not – and once a safe distance from your home, you remember you left your favorite electronic game behind.

I missed the seasons, even the cold ones. We'd had five Christmas' in space, traveling through the sky like lost vacationers with no idea of where we were going. We'd managed a tree out of an iron pipe, and decorations from clothing that was worn out, cut into tiny pieces. We'd gathered pieces of wire no longer in use to hang the colored fabric, and the best leftover throw-away containers you've ever seen for awkward looking ornaments.

Presents consisted of love notes and nice things we had thought up to do for others. It was pretty boring, I can tell you, but sort of nice in a strange way. I mean, we were going to have to be with these people for a long time, maybe even forever before we found a planet that could support life.

As it was, Mom was always trying and failing to make things just like home, and Dad, well, let's just say he was working on one thing or another. There was a map, an electronic thing that could light up an entire room upon touch, and technical gizmos that had been difficult to fabricate up in space. Many of my favorites had been broken upon re-entry to Earth (when the shuttle hadn't been able to escape the planet and had crash-landed before my family had finally met up with them), and so parts and pieces had to be scrounged up and fitted together, even if the pieces didn't exactly fit.

Somehow, we'd managed in the space plane, and the advancements discovered on board hadn't hurt us any, including keeping the craft going beyond its expected landing port. I wasn't sure about all of the details, mainly because none of the adults talked about it outside of the 'room.'

But we'll get to that later.

I was bored out of my mind most days. If it wasn't for Neva and Stella and the green stone, I would have gone crazy. But wouldn't you know it, the day I thought I'd lost it for sure, yelling at Barina, (the one who had first met us when we reached Space Doc 5), something fantastic was discovered in the ink-black sky I would never forget.

Dwarf Star

It was red.

"A dwarf star," Dad said. "Smaller and fainter in brilliance than what you're used to but stronger in warmth than you might expect."

I looked over at Stella. "You mean that red star will support all of the planets?"

"Not all of them. Just three."

Neva sat on my shoulders like always. The green stone was in my pocket. Although I had spoken to Neva about the end of the world, told him about my fears, my boredom, I still hadn't had many reasons to use the green stone. There was only one wall that was worth traveling within.

And now there was a red star and three planets that would support life. After five years we were here.

Mom had a small tear dripping from her left eye. She was blinking like there was no tomorrow. But there would be a tomorrow after all.

"You can't go down yet," Dad said, pushing me lightly on the shoulder. We were in a holding pattern, near planet one, and I couldn't believe it.

"Your dad's right."

"But you said there was air, oxygen, that everything's been tested."

Neva hopped down and looked up at me. "Listen, Aaden."

"I'm tired of listening, and I'm tired of being in this place!" I was fifteen, although I still looked ten, and I think most people, especially the adults, forgot about that. I would never age, would always look the same. My parents would never get old either, and they were grateful, something I could actually understand.

I thought of the green stone but didn't lift it from my pocket. Instead, I looked over at Mom, really looked at her. She seemed tired, sadder than I'd ever seen her. I didn't understand it. We were here – here!

"I want to go," I said.

Mom shuffled her feet and took me in her arms. I felt stupid. "We aren't the first ones to arrive on this planet," she whispered. She looked up at Neva briefly.

"Why am I always the last one to know anything?" I asked, trying to release myself.

"We couldn't tell you until we were sure about some things."

"What things?"

Neva hopped on my shoulder and stroked my neck with his wet fingers. "I can't believe you guys. So, there are others on the planet. So What? Do they have purple skin or something?"

"No," Dad said.

"Then what?" I managed to extricate myself from Mom.

"They are a war-faring race."

I couldn't believe it. Neither Stella nor Neva would be able to handle it if we lived there. "What about planet number two?" I asked. *I knew I sounded like an old game show – Do you want door number one, two or three?* But I didn't care. I just needed to plant my feet on solid ground.

Stella smiled up at me. "I heard that," she said. "Don't worry, your dad will be fine and then he'll come back for us. All of the planets are at war."

I couldn't believe it, but then again, I could. What did people always do when they wanted power; when they thought they were better than others? War. Even Earth had had its share of wars; wars that had miraculously stopped when everyone discovered that they were all going to die anyway.

I blinked my eyes, wiped a stray tear that I didn't even know was there and sat down. "Okay," I said, "check out the planet, but I want to be the next one off this plane."

Dad smiled over at me as if I was telling a joke. He wore the same silver suit, mended and cleaned from those days five years ago on Earth, and it was almost as if my time on Earth hadn't happened. But my time there had been real, and the memories would always be a part of me.

What would the people on this faraway planet have to say about us? Would they like us, or would we be hated on their first inspection? I remembered my first thoughts of Neva, and I wondered how different the people that populated this planet would be.

Someone landed the plane, it was probably Barina or one of her compatriots. Bronty had been lain to rest a year ago, been placed in a pod and sent off into the stars. The amazing thing was, before that, as we traveled through the skies, Bronty had grown younger. Just a day before his passing (he'd reached the ripe old age of 25), something had gone wrong. I'd never expected Bronty to travel back in time; age-wise that is, but when it happened, he was all I could talk about. I knew that very soon Bronty and I would be the same age, and that we would be able to do stuff like we used to – even play Legos if we wanted to re-invent them.

When Bronty got sick, I thought it was just a cold or something. And when he died, I thought maybe I was dreaming and that I would wake up any second. But the second passed, and then the next and the next, and Bronty didn't return to life.

I hated Bronty for that. All he'd been able to think about was saving the world, forgetting me entirely. But then again, I was a part of the world, and I could have been a part of the destruction if Neva and Stella hadn't saved my family, and if the others near the space plane and shuttle hadn't had their own alien species called Triumph to protect them.

Traveling for five years had given me ample time to figure it out. When the sun burned like hot lava, Neva and Stella felt it almost as warmly as I did. They needed sap. But there was a problem with that too. The soil had been damaged because of the planet's destruction, making everything die almost on contact. The good news? Both of my friends had evolved from needing the soil and so could avoid sure death by merely breathing in the oxygen that still surrounded the planet – at least for a time.

I remembered when Mom wanted to shelter her talking plants during the winter; she used mulch and burlap and covered the crying plants through the winter. Most of them lived through it. It was the covering that finally gave scientists the answers to changing the habitat of plants, though they could never see the plants as being equal to humans. In time, however, the monophylum had figured it out for themselves. What made them tick had nothing to do with brains and tissues and blood, but everything to do with the sun. They were able to create their own ethereal barrier after that.

After Dad went down to the surface, a sort of red-orange planet that could barely be seen because of the heavy clouds surrounding it, I went to my room that was more like a closet and began to gather my things. There wasn't much: a set of clothes, (too worn out to even be called clothes), my voice-activated flashlight and water jug, and a few wires I'd managed to scrounge up and make into things like alien creatures and space planes.

Rushing to the 'room', I hoped to see Barina. We sort of had this love-hate relationship. I hated that she'd left my family behind in the first place but loved her because she'd finally saved us all. There were nine of us on the space plane; we'd begun with ten.

"Barina!" Barina turned from the space console and stared at me. "How did you get in here?" she asked.

I shrugged my shoulders and caressed the green stone in my pocket. It was amazing how long it had taken me to figure that one out.

"Your father needs all of the attention we can give him now," she said, turning to the console. It had gadgets on it that I could only dream of using.

"I don't see anything," I said, and I meant it. I'd even snuck in here at nights the last couple of years, more times than I could count, with little to show for it. But I knew a couple of things. I knew how to light up the console, and I knew that one of the gadgets allowed a person to be transported to the surface.

I could see by the map that we were by a planet – the blue dot was visible now next to a dot that represented a planet. But the mark was just a dot and I was disappointed yet again. The console wasn't much to look at, and that news hadn't changed since the first time I'd tried to work it.

"I can show you the console later. For now, …" Barina brushed her black hair from her face. "For now, prepare yourself like the others are doing."

"Where is my mom?"

"Getting ready as you should be," Barina said. "Why don't you see what Neva and Stella are doing?"

"Maybe I can help you?"

"You're not old enough. Besides…" Barina's blue eyes stared me down, and I suddenly felt uncomfortable, "what you need to do is relax. It will be many hours yet before you'll get the opportunity to walk on the surface of the planet."

Suddenly a slimy hand reached out to me and directed me to the doorway.

"Triumph!" I wailed.

"Barina's right. Let's get you to your room."

"I thought you were on my side." I knew Triumph wasn't, but this particular monophylum had a screw loose or something, and I loved to tease him. He didn't look a bit like Neva or Stella, having grown in the lusher area of Taurus, and considered himself privileged and a better breed of plant than the two I'd grown to love.

"I *am* on your side." Triumph continued to pull me to the doorway. The door opened, then closed behind us. I walked with hesitation to my room.

Meteor Shower

You need to know that I didn't stay long in my room, but every time I tried to retreat, Triumph blocked me. He was a conniving monophylum, and I wondered how long it would take him to fall asleep so that I could check things out.

Monophyla, whether like Triumph or not, didn't need the sleep I did, but I did my best to stay alert until I knew he would be asleep. I paced the room mostly, and ate, and waited for my mom to come and tell me it was time to turn off the light.

When she entered near midnight, she looked at me with drooping eyes, kissed me once on the cheek, and retreated to her sleeping quarters which adjoined mine. I didn't ask about Dad, but I knew what her answer would be.

I sat still on my bed for some time watching the clock. When it finally read 2 a.m., I re-dressed and tiptoed to the door. In an instant the door *whirred* open and I stood outside. Just as I suspected, Triumph had finally *caved* and gone to bed.

I laughed at my little joke and retreated down the hall to 'the room.' The wall opened easily, and I retreated inside, the wall closing behind me. I went right to the console and pushed the button Barina had used to get the screen to light up. Sure enough, the silver dial lit up for me, and in seconds I was seeing the blinking blue light. Everything must have been on autopilot, because I couldn't see anyone else in 'the room', and wondered how long I had until Barina – the one who usually flew the plane – would return.

What I did next could only be interpreted as madness.

Pushing one button and then another to see what the plane would do, I finally managed to get the shaking to stop, and the port to open. The rattling of the plane, for only a few brief seconds, scared me out of my wits, but no one came inside, and I was allowed to continue my investigation.

If you've ever watched *Star Trek* – any of the Generations – you'll know how I felt to see the floor light up just in front of the console. It not only lit up but blinked wildly. I had never seen anyone transported to the surface before – because there'd not been anything to transport to – but I'd listened to about everything there was to hear from the three men and two women, not including my parents, who delighted in speaking too loud about how smart they were.

And now that we were circling a new world, their mouths had become even more open and revealing than those I recognized in Neva and Stella, who were more than likely asleep now too, though the thought of leaving them behind didn't feel right. I was afraid to go on my own.

Once the blinking stopped, I figured it was time, but I wasn't really sure of anything. What I knew most of all is that I couldn't stay here and that I needed to find my dad before the murderous creatures down there did.

How long did it take for diplomacy? To check everything out on the surface?

I had a sick feeling inside that my dad's entrance into this new world had been anything but positive. Why else hadn't anyone said a word?

Stepping from the console, I stood in the bright heat of the yellow light and closed my eyes. Nothing happened. And then, I could feel the stone in my pocket. It was on fire.

I pulled it from my pocket and looked down at it. The stone was red.

I don't know how I managed it, but maybe I did. Suddenly, a portal opened into the sky and I was outside the space plane, soaring to the ground like a meteor. It was freaky I can tell you. I was my own ball of fire. I passed the clouds that hovered above the red planet, zipped past the space plane as if it was nothing, and made my way to the surface, my face burning from the speed of descent.

Nearing the surface, which felt more like hell now that I was close to it, I closed my eyes and took in my last breath.

Only it wasn't my last breath, but more like swimming under the water and then, quite suddenly, it happened. I found myself on the surface, taking in that well-needed breath of air.

I breathed in. I breathed out. I coughed – once.

Looking around me, I appeared to be alone, though I was laying on my back and could only see up. I heard nothing but my pounding heart. For surely, it was pounding, and my breath was uneven, and my eyes blinked up at the other side of the thick clouds.

But what was that? A sun. No, a red dwarf star. The air was fairly hot, at least 100 degrees, and I couldn't see anything other than dirt to the right and left of me in the darkened morning.

I sat up slowly, not really trusting my breathing, but knowing I had to trust it. What else could I do? With the help of the green stone, I had managed to transport myself onto a barren planet inhabited by who knows what kind of alien race. But I had done it.

I had done it.

The Red Planet

You know what it feels like that first time you walk into school alone, that first day when you're at a new school and don't know anyone yet? Or, there's this girl – who is always staring at you, but says nothing?

Well, that's how I felt. Weirded out. I could have been in the middle of a warrior fight, or even a stare down, and I would have felt more comfortable. As it was, I stood a bit shakily and looked around me.

I saw nothing but straggly trees, brownish plants, and dirt – red dirt. No water, but suddenly I was very, very thirsty. There were no mountains like I was used to, only flatness, like the bottom of a hand or shoe, like the bottom of a sea.

Why was I thinking of that again?

I blinked and walked from where I had landed, taking each step slowly, watching, always watching. The air was silent. I didn't hear any birds; I didn't see any creatures on the ground. I took out the stone from my pocket. It had returned to the green color I knew and glowed iridescently in the darkness. So, it would suffice as a flashlight, too.

Still, I hadn't prepared myself for this. Unlike my first journey to save my parents and to find a way off Earth, this time, I'd acted hastily, too hastily. I had no food. No water. But I had the green stone. That had to count for something. And I'd made it here. I'd made it.

I don't know when I slept, but when I was awakened, it was because of a loud booming sound. At first, I reached for my pillow, and then, finding nothing but dirt, sat up, only to discover I was no longer alone.

"Don't be afraid," Neva whispered on my shoulder. "I'm here."

"Neva? Stella?"

Neva jumped off and stood in front of me. Neva and Stella were of the cornstalk variety, their ancestry dating back to the days when corn was grown in the heat of summer and gathered in late fall. But when the corn had begun to dry up, and the knowledge of what they could become had begun to seep into their minds like manna from heaven, they had left the confines of the ground once and for all with a promise to themselves and to each other, that they would never be bound again.

"How did you get here?" I asked, knowing full well that he'd jumped on my shoulder just in time to be transported here by the power of the green stone.

"You know."

"Where is Stella?"

"Here."

I jumped. "Where?"

"On your other shoulder." In seconds I could see her standing next to Neva. They clasped hands.

"Why?" I asked.

"We knew what you were going to do, so we took care of high and mighty Triumph, so you could make your way here."

"How did you…"

"Easy…" I was suddenly dizzy.

Neva sat, and motioned me to join him. "We kept him busy with facts and figures like he's used to."

"Figures," I said, and laughed at my own joke.

"You'll need invisibility," Stella offered, "and plenty of help staying on track." She closed her mouth abruptly, but I knew what she meant. I'd forgotten all of the necessary things one needed to travel on an unknown planet, and instead, had remembered one of my wire projects. I pulled it from my pocket now and stretched out the wings. I couldn't help it, metal or not, the blue wire reminded me of Earth.

Neva smiled up at me.

"I see you haven't forgotten the most important things," he said.

I looked down at Neva's crooked smile and had to laugh. "I'm thirsty, though," I said, trying not to give myself too big of a guilt trip. I was pretty good at those.

"We figured that," Stella said, removing a small pack from her back and opening it up. She reached inside and produced a small, metal container.

"Water?" I asked.

"Even better." She pushed open the lid and handed the container to me. It was as light as air.

I poured the contents into my mouth without another thought, and then, just as suddenly, gagged. Spitting out the juices, I turned my eyes to both of them. What were they trying to do, poison me?

"I know what you're thinking, but water mixed with sap can be a really good thing. We promise."

Stella blinked over at me, her one green eye opening and closing about five times. If I hadn't known any better, I might have thought she was flirting with me. Yes, my body looked to be about ten, my natural age, but my soul was anything but ten. I'd started to think about girls, and not in the way I used to if you get my drift. I sort of wanted to meet one. Not an old one, but a younger one like me that could understand what I was going through. But there had been no one on board for the past five years who was any younger than Barina – and she would be forever twenty-five.

I'd discovered her true age that first year in flight when she'd begun to look on me as a brother, and all I wanted to do was escape her piercing eyes. I felt like her favorite doll or something. By the time we'd reached our second year, she'd practically adopted me as her own.

But maybe that was because I was sort of close to her age, or young enough to still understand what younger people liked. What I know for sure is that by the third year, she had taken me into confidence.

Through our question and answer sessions, I'd managed to retrieve some pretty reliable information about the spacecraft without her being aware of it. And I'd managed to get her confidence when it came to keeping secrets. I hadn't told anyone on board what I knew, though I'm sure the word about what she had shared with me would have made its rounds soon enough if I'd said something.

But now I was here on the red planet, with the burning red star that served as the sun. And it was hot. How could it be night and still be so hot?

When I awoke, it was with the same star blasting. I sat and felt for the metal container. Opening the lid, I drained the remaining juices, disgusting as they were. Stella and Neva were already awake though the sky was still dark.

"How long did I sleep?" I asked.

Neva's eye burned into mine. "Too long," he said. "We need to move to the nearest place of water."

"Where's that?"

Stella pointed. "There is more than likely some water underground, but nothing above." She gave a sideways glance to Neva.

It was hotter than blazes. "What time is it?" I asked.

"Morning. Near 5 a.m. Earth time."

"Why is it so hot?"

Stella nodded to Neva. "It's time to go," she said. "We'll tell you on the way."

I tried to smile, but the heat was bearing down on me like a hundred she-goats. Milk... now that sounded good. We'd even been able to fabricate the taste and color on the space plane, but never well enough. I still missed the milk at home.

"Can you protect us from the heat?" I asked. "I'm sweating bullets."

"Only for a time," Neva offered. "We must conserve our strength."

In moments the memories returned of my last days on Earth, and the protection we'd received from Neva right before the blast of Mercury and Mars. I would be forever grateful for the shielded protection that day, just as I was suddenly feeling thankful now.

"Thank you," I said, walking the course to who-knows-where. There wasn't an alien in sight, not a green plant, not anything but the baking soil on a planet with a red star.

"You may want to disguise us," I said.

"Invisibility on top of protection from the elements?"

I nodded. If what my friends said was true, it was only a matter of time before we were noticed and dragged somewhere, bound and tied.

But Neva and Stella were silent. "Didn't you hear me?" I finally asked. "And what about the space plane? Barina has to know we have left the ship."

"She knows."

"Well, maybe she will save us."

"She can't."

"Why not? All she has to do is use the transporter. I've seen it. I know what it does."

Stella looked at me quizzically.

"Really, Aaden. The flares?"

"What flares?"

"You only survived because of the stone. The others would have a terrible time making it down here without the stone's help."

"What about my dad?"

"He took a chance."

"A chance?" I gasped. "Then, he could be dead?"

"It's likely," Stella said, "but we won't know for sure until we get closer."

"The magnetic fields keep many from this planet," Neva offered, though it was hard for me to concentrate on him. I thought about never seeing my dad again. I thought of the stupid choice I'd made coming here with no plan other than to save him.

Looking up from the red ground I tried to focus my eyes on what might be out in the distance, and suddenly it was there. Something I remembered.

The Pillar of Delhi

We must have walked for miles before I stopped to rest. By then, I'd heard the story of the 'almost' capture, the reasons why those who lived here spent most of their time underground, the gigantic flares that would more than likely take the skin off me if any one of them ever landed within even inches of me, and the story of where my dad was kept prisoner.

But I'm getting ahead of myself again, and so we'll start with the most important fact: My dad was being held in the city of Delhi. Neva had heard him speaking into the air like a lone ghost.

I was terrified. I had no idea what was going to happen next or what these aliens looked like. I hoped they were small and harmless like Neva and Stella. But I knew they could also be giants, larger than life creatures that sucked blood, or worse, ate you in one bite.

"Make yourself invisible," Neva said.

I knew that I could drift in and out of solid stone walls, I even knew that the green stone had allowed me to come without injury to this planet, but make myself disappear? I didn't have the power to do that. Invisibility was Neva's deal – Stella's.

"You also have the power. Do it – now!"

I took out the stone. It glowed green in my hand, and suddenly, before I knew what was happening, I could no longer see my feet.

"Wow!" I gasped.

"Now, keep quiet. We must make it to the pillar. We cannot be discovered."

I breathed a deep sigh and felt something like a finger against my lips.

"Silence!" Neva said into my mind. "From now on, while we are without the walls, telekinesis is our only option." So that's what it was called, such a strange name for such a powerful gift.

I nodded, not seeing either Neva or Stella, but knowing they were there.

We approached the pillar and all I could think about was how incredible it was that there were two of them. One on what used to be Earth, and one here, on the red planet. Time seemed to stand still as we approached the pillar. Though the air was hot, and the land empty of anything of real worth, I felt only protection.

The pillar stood before us like a giant finger. I looked up. Someone or some 'thing' had managed to carve what looked like four hats on top. That sounds funny, I know, but they looked like hats. The first hat, nearest the base, was carved with horizontal lines, the second and third hat's edges were carved like scalloped curtains, the last, like a cap you'd wear upon graduation. Only there wasn't a tassel. It would have seemed funny to me at any other time, but not now. Now, it was like the pillar was speaking to me. I could see quite plainly, what looked like engravings on the iron walls, symbols only those of this alien race would be able to read; circles and lines, hooks and branches.

It was weird, I tell you, so weird that I wasn't listening when I should have been.

In an instant, I was pulled to the ground. I could see my feet. The stone I'd been holding was glittering on the red ground, and above me was a girl.

She was slight, hardly bigger than Neva and Stella, but she was taller and her hair was yellow; bright yellow like the sun. Like a lemon, like a spark of fire before it kindles to red.

She was human.

"My name is Chandra," said the girl with the lighting hair. "Come with me."

An invisible door which had somehow opened and allowed us in – smelled of wet leaves and grass as if someone had just mowed the lawn. Yes, we were still known to do that on Earth, though robots had taken over the task for the most part.

Chandra didn't acknowledge Neva or Stella, and I wondered if she could see them, but in time, only moments from that first moment I saw her, I knew that she could. And here's something you don't hear every day. She *knew* them.

I guess I shouldn't have been surprised, heck, these two always had things hidden up their sleeves (in a manner of speaking) that I only discovered at the last moment, why wouldn't they keep the knowledge of this planet and the beings that inhabited it, a secret?

I followed Chandra through the dark tunnel, lit only by the light that came from the stone – the green stone Chandra had offered me soon after I gasped at her presence. "You will need this," she'd said, and she was right. As I followed her down the dark and endless tunnel, that crisscrossed and maneuvered its way like a giant snake, all I could do was follow.

Neva and Stella were as silent as death anyway, and, though I knew they were there, Neva didn't speak into my ear, even silently, as I thought he should, and Stella was about as talkative as a strand of yellow hair.

I looked at that hair now and could hardly believe my eyes. I didn't want to stare at it; what would she know if I did anyway, unless, like my mother, she had eyes in the back of her head, in a manner of speaking. I couldn't see any, either figuratively or literally, and I was glad of that. She looked human, had to be human, and I could hardly believe my fortune.

Okay, so I suddenly liked girls. And no, I wasn't going to tell her how I was feeling. That would be stupid. Though I was fifteen, I still looked ten, and this girl, why, she had to be at least fourteen, maybe older. It was hard to tell if you know what I mean.

I jumped and blinked at her when she stopped and looked back.

"What?" I offered.

"Follow me," she blinked. Her eyes were green, the color of the stone.

I breathed, trying not to let it show, any of it. How I liked how she looked, and how I hoped she wasn't taking us somewhere to be eaten alive.

A giggle escaped her lips, it must have, but she didn't turn back.

We followed until the last opening revealed light.

"See, we have arrived," she said.

I blinked. Before me sat a table and four chairs made out of wood. On top were three bowls. I didn't smell anything, but I was suddenly hungry.

"Sit."

Finding the nearest chair, I sat. Neva and Stella found chairs of their own, leaving Chandra with the only chair without a bowl in front of it.

"Goldilocks?" I asked.

"What?"

"Never mind." I looked down. Well, it sure looked like hot cereal. Looking to the right, I picked up the spoon. "Do you have any sugar?" I asked.

"What?" Chandra answered, staring me down with her sparkling green eyes.

Suddenly I couldn't stand it, any of it. I looked over at Neva. He was grinning crookedly. And Stella? Something funny was going on...

"Wait!" Stella peered over at me.

"You have a bite first," I said, looking directly at Chandra. "If you don't die, we'll be safe."

Handing her the spoon, which also was wooden, I placed the bowl in front of her.

That's when the most incredible, frightening thing happened. If I hadn't seen something close to it, just days before, I would have jumped right out of my skin.

A purple tongue pushed out of her small mouth and lapped at the hot cereal like there was no tomorrow.

I reached for the bowl. Forgetting the spoon, I sunk my face into what was left of the warm cereal. Yep, it was just like the hot cereal I was used to eating and I was past hungry. It tasted just right.

More than likely you're laughing at this. I know I would be. Some girl with yellow hair and green eyes had sucked up almost the entire bowl of cereal and with a purple tongue no less.

"Who are you?" I asked, wiping my mouth with my sleeve.

"I told you." She peered over at Neva and Stella. "Thank you for bringing him." Neva grinned solidly now, his crooked smile filling much of his green face. Stella was doing the same.

"Who are you?" I asked again.

"You'd better show him," Neva answered.

"Oh, alright, but I was having so much fun."

At that moment, Chandra revealed herself, green skin and all.

"So, you're…"

"Just like your friends."

"Except you're wearing clothes," I offered.

She brushed at the purple jumpsuit of sorts she was wearing. Her feet were bare.

"I am the guardian," she said.

I didn't sleep. Though Chandra had finally allowed me some sleep, bringing in bedding and something like a pillow to lay my head on, all I could think about was being alone. Neva and Stella were no longer with me.

The place was cool, though not cold, and reminded me a little of the caves I'd left on Earth. Except the walls didn't glow with green stones or brown or back ones for that matter. The walls were like clear stones, like a mirror. I couldn't see myself through them, but the wall appeared like glass.

Do you know how silent it gets in the mountains, especially in the winter? When all you can hear is your footsteps tromping through the snow, or the crackling of branches? Well, this was how silent it was in the room where I was trying to sleep. It was like the dead of winter had come.

The stone lit up the room some, and I knew I could walk without the walls with the stone's use, but where would I go? What would I do? Better to stay here, in this strange place, at least for the night.

I sat, bolting upright. The screech up the corridor was deafening, like a bear gone mad. In seconds, I was thinking of the bear that had somehow managed to escape the destruction of Earth and the way Mom had calmed me so that I wouldn't be eaten.

I looked to my right and left but kept my body still. I couldn't smell anything – see anything – although what had once been darkness was now like the light dawning. There were no windows, and yet, the place was definitely lighter than when I'd finally fallen asleep.

The mad bear shrieking continued. I covered my ears.

"Neva! Stella!" I screamed inside my head.

Nothing.

"Neva! Stel –"

"Shhhhh, listennnnn. The others have come."

"What others?"

"Listennnnn."

Sitting still on my bed, I managed to uncover my ears. The ringing had stopped.

"We have been taken."

I stood from the bed and walked to the entrance. The entire walkway was lit up as if by some invisible force.

"Where?"

"They will find you. You will be taken. Hide the stone."

I looked toward the bed, picked up the green stone, and looked for a place to hide it within the walls. There was nothing; no grooves, no holes. Neva must be crazy! I didn't even have a pack to hide it inside!

Twisting the stone within my hands I thought about going within the walls. Yes, that would do it. I would escape into the walls, hide there with it, and search for Neva and Stella on my own terms. Taking the stone into my hands I drifted inside and turned to face the room. Amazingly, I could see what I'd just left. It was empty. But no, someone or some 'thing' had just entered.

It was hairy like a bear, though it wasn't exactly a bear. It stood on two legs, like a circus bear from the olden days, and spoke with a raspy voice, like something solid was caught inside its throat. The head was small, far too small for its big body, and the eyes were a piercing red, like a set of tail lights.

"I know you're here," the beast said, though I'd thought to remain hidden inside the walls, the green stone quickly hidden for security in my pant pocket. "I know you're here. I see you."

"What?" I said suddenly, forgetting myself.

The bear thing smiled. It had large pointed teeth, far too white in my opinion, and a strange way of walking as it approached the wall. Suddenly, and before I could react, the hairy beast had drawn me out without even a touch. In only seconds, it had pulled me from the wall.

"That's better," the beast said, pushing me to the ground with, what appeared to be, merely a look of its eyes. "Give me the stone."

I looked up at the bear-beast, tears glistening. So, this, or something like it, had captured my friends and I was next.

"Now!" The thing roared, and I covered my ears. This, indeed, was a bear of the worst sort.

I shook my head.

"It's in your pocket!"

Again, I shook my head. The thing, whatever it was, would have to kill me before I'd give it the stone.

But the beast just stood there, blinking its red eyes at me. I could feel its sweet breath, like decaying fruit.

"W-what have you done with m-my friends?" I managed.

"Give me the stone, and I will reply to your question." The beast sat on the edge of the bed. I was still standing. It was taller than me.

"You'll have to grab it from my dead corpse," I said bravely.

The thing smirked. "Hand it to me!" it shrieked.

At that moment I thought of something, and the thought gave me hope. If I didn't give the beast the stone, would it be able to take it from me?

"No!" I shouted.

The beast reached for me, and then, just as suddenly, recoiled. It looked afraid. How was that possible? I was less than half its size!

"If you give me the stone, you will see your friends again. If not, they will die."

"You can't have it."

The beast stood to its full height and screamed that infuriating scream. I covered my ears.

"Then your friends will die!" The beast returned to the front opening, walking in a sort of stop and go fashion. I wasn't sure what it reminded of me then, but now I think I can tell you. It was like a mechanical toy; you know the wind-up ones that were long gone even before my mom was born. I could see its tail from the back, a short little thing, just like I'd seen on the bears back on Earth. Was he some sort of advanced bear, just like Neva and Stella were advanced plants?

"Wait!" I shouted, fumbling for the green stone. Pulling it from my pocket, I held it up.

"Now, there's a good boy!" The beast smiled, its white teeth gleaming. It reached its paw toward me, though not as close as before.

"I will give you the stone on one condition," I said.

"And what is that?"

"Take me to my friends. If they are safe and unhurt, the stone is yours."

It was the biggest lie I'd ever told another person, human or not, but I had a plan, and this plan would help me in both departments.

The Yellow Room

I'd never been interrogated before, but this must have come close to it. The yellow room held no furniture. I sat in the corner, and the bear-thing hovered above me like an eerie street light on Halloween.

Yes, we'd still celebrate Halloween, even on the space plane, and I was glad of it. Some things in life were simply too good to forget. Like Christmas, Halloween was at the top of my *bucket* list (no pun intended).

Anyway, as I looked into the red eyes of the beast, I waited or tried to wait patiently, for my friends to arrive. After a while, the beast spoke:

"It may take some time. They are at the other end of the catacombs. You still have the stone?"

I reached inside my pocket and felt for the thin line. Strangely, it calmed me.

"Hold it up," the beast offered.

"Tell me your name," I asked.

"Grude," it said. "I am the prime of my kind."

"Oh," I said, trying not to fidget.

"I am the largest. I am respected for my power and authority."

"What sort of power?" I asked, pushing myself up against the wall of yellow glass.

"You saw it. I can wield with only my thoughts."

"Oh, that."

"You are not impressed? Show me the stone."

I lifted the stone from my pocket and placed it slightly in front of my body.

"I can't believe I am the first to see it. The others, they will see that I have the power to wield – even this."

"You didn't do anything," I offered. "I found the stone, I brought it here to this…this red planet."

The beast smiled. "And I captured you, and in time, I will have what rightly belongs to me."

In that instant, the room filled with other beasts like Grude, though smaller than my smelly companion. There were six of them, and behind them, shackled with some sort of clear twine – stood my friends.

Neva blinked, and I could see that Stella had been crying.

"How are you?" I asked in my mind.

"How do we look?" Neva offered back.

"Quiet!" Grude pulled my two friends in front of it with its eyes. So, the beast had heard the conversation, and, if the conversation, then more than likely he knew of my plan to escape with my friends.

"Too noisy, all of you!" The beast shrieked and I covered my ears.

The others smiled. They had the same white teeth, and the yellow room was beginning to smell like an orchard of decaying fruit.

"The stone."

I reached inside my pocket, placed my fingers around the green stone and felt for the calming line, the crack that illuminated everything. Shutting my eyes, I didn't speak, not even in my thoughts.

Though the beast had suddenly jumped forward, the dome of protection was around me and my friends even before I'd consciously thought about it. Reaching for my friends, I pulled them inside.

Anger filled the room. It was like a planet had hit.

"We will only be safe for a time," Neva said, hopping on my left shoulder.

Stella took the other. "We must move fast," she said.

In a second thought, but probably before the thought had entered my brain, we were outside the underground catacombs. It was still early out as if the sun was just rising, but I knew it wasn't that – would never be that. This planet didn't have a sun, just a red star that burned hotter than the sun I knew.

"Take us to your space plane," Chandra offered suddenly. "We must move, and quick!"

"But my dad!" Escape had been part of my plan, but not this!

"There is nothing we can do for him now," Chandra said, taking my hand. Her hand was wet, and I knew that even though she had changed back into the girl I'd first discovered, for what reason I wasn't exactly sure of, there was no way I was going to return to the space plane without my dad.

I turned to the Iron Pillar of Delphi. It had just slid open, revealing the face of Grude.

"Now!" Chandra said.

We were protected by the stone, but I had no idea how long that would be. In a blink, maybe less, the decision had been made. In the next, I wondered why I had made it. I also wondered how I'd been able to bring everyone with me. I just knew that I could.

In the whirr of return, I felt the heat on my face. And suddenly, there was a distinct pinch as something drew near my legs. And then a voice, a voice I knew well, spoke.

"Son! I thought you were dead!" Mom's voice suddenly hovered next to mine like a flowering plant. We were back on the space plane and I knew her even before I saw her. "What were you thinking?"

I blinked over at her and placed the green stone back in my pocket.

Chandra must have been doing something extraordinary because Mom's eyes turned directly to her after she made sure that I was well. "And you, who are you?"

I looked to my right. Chandra was still in the fake girl's getup. "You need to change," I said. "Now."

"Oh, do I have to? I sort of like being human."

Mom's eyes bored from her head. They might have fallen out if they hadn't been connected by tissue from behind. "Yes, I think I'd like to see that," she said.

Chandra smiled once and the change was made.

"Well, something about this doesn't surprise me," Mom said, looking down at Neva and Stella, and staring at Chandra once again. "You two, were you in on this?"

"Just barely," Stella offered. "Your son needed some protection, and we were in the right place at the right time."

I looked back at Mom. She still had an angry look in her eyes. Just beside her was Barina. The look she gave Stella and Neva was anything but cheerful. "You can't be trusted." She looked at me, and her voice softened. "We promised your mother that you wouldn't escape again."

"Is that what you think I did? Escape? I went in search of Dad."

Chandra moved uneasily beside me. I could feel it, though I didn't look at her directly. "I'm sorry Aaden, your father is gone," she said, though I wasn't sure if the words came the natural way or not. I was getting used to speaking inside my head.

"Listen…" Chandra touched me again on the hand. I looked down at her. "Your father was with the others."

"With who? Grude?"

She nodded. "Their kind have no mercy, especially for humans."

"So, he was there with us – underground?"

"Dead. No human, no matter how expert, no matter how clever, can survive the planet surface without the help of the stone. He was taken down with the others soon after he was discovered."

I looked at Mom. Her lips trembled.

Darkened

Before sneaking over to 'the room' I went over the details of what I knew for sure. First, creatures like Grude were the only ones who could survive indefinitely on the surface of the red planet without the stone. They could hear my thoughts, and they had a strength to move through walls, even without the power of the stone.

But they obviously weren't too smart. Why bring all of my friends together if Grude knew my thoughts and escape plans?

Maybe the answer would come in time. Just like the secret of where my Dad was. If he was dead, buried in some unknown grave on the planet's surface, I would find him. And, if alive, I would find him.

Sitting up from my bed, I packed the last jug of water – I had five – planted the green stone back inside my pocket and reached for my jacket. Searching the room, all was still. Though Mom was in the next, she had fallen asleep soon after she'd lectured me. I wasn't sure where Chandra was, but I didn't need her help, nor the help of Neva and Stella.

Opening the door, I was met with a green eye, the green eye of Triumph.

"What do you think you are doing?" he asked.

"You see me?" I offered.

"Of course. Pull out the green stone."

I pulled the stone from my pocket. Amazingly, the stone was black.

"You have used all of its power."

"Oh." The thought occurred to me for the first time, that this was more than likely why no one had taken it from me. But when had it changed? Why hadn't I noticed that it was black when I'd placed it in my pocket just moments before?

"You were too busy thinking of your escape," Triumph offered. "You are always thinking too much, and not listening."

I glared down at him. "And you'll always be a plant!" I shouted, turning from the door, and going back inside my room.

I sat on the bed and looked down at the dark stone. "How could you do this to me?" I asked it.

"*You* did it."

I jumped like a firecracker had hit me on the backside. Mom knew all about firecrackers from her childhood. By the time I was born they'd been banned in favor of glowing flashlights that were light as a feather and never needed batteries.

"What did you say?"

"You – did it. You used me up on that planet, and now I'll need to recharge. The others know how much time you have, and they are resting a while until I turn back on."

"And when is that?" I asked.

"I cannot tell you."

"Why not?"

"The answer is obvious."

"But you are my... rock."

"Not yet."

"I'm fifteen!"

"You act ten."

I glared down at the stone. "So, what do you know? I might look ten, but I'm fifteen."

The stone was silent.

"So?" I prodded.

But the stone didn't speak.

The next morning, before I'd opened my eyes, Chandra was in my room. She was in human form.

"How did you sleep?" she asked, twirling her yellow hair between her thumb and forefinger.

"Wouldn't you like to know," I answered, sitting up. The stone was still at my side. It was still black. Chandra was wearing purple, the same purple outfit that managed to fit her body when she also turned back into a monophylum.

"Why do you do that?" I asked.

"Change? Human form suits me."

"But your hair is too yellow."

"Is it?"

"Too yellow. Your face is too perfect."

"You like my green eyes?"

"Eye," I corrected.

Chandra frowned. "Why don't you like me like this?" she asked.

"It's fake," I answered, though the real truth was that I really did like her in human form.

Chandra smiled suddenly. "You need to be more careful," she said. "You really do like me."

I must have blushed, but Chandra didn't say anything.

"You need to wait for the stone to turn green, don't you remember?"

I did, though much of my time on Earth I was trying to block out. The experience down there had been just too painful. I'd been blinded by the stone. I'd had to wait to be healed. I'd had to wait for the stone to 'power-up'. And then something else came to me. I began to remember how important thinking good thoughts were in the use of my gifts and how faith was a part of it, too.

"You have been conflicted in your thoughts," Chandra whispered as if speaking the same words loudly would damage them somehow.

"Conflicted?" I offered, though I was pretty sure what the word meant.

"Where is your focus now? On saving your father? On getting to the planet so you can live out the life you want? What?"

"What do you care?" I punched the bed.

"See what I mean?" Chandra stood, walking to the other side of the room. I watched as the length of her purple covering slid on the floor behind her. It was the first time I realized she was wearing some sort of short wedding train, like brides, only the train was purple and not lace or something else stupid.

"I heard that."

Chandra turned and blinked both green eyes at me. "I have always wanted to be human, even before I knew of their existence," she said.

"That's impossible."

"You think so now, but there are many things I knew about before they happened."

"Like what?" I glared at her, trying not to blink my eyes.

"Like you, for example. I knew you were coming to save us even before you showed yourself."

"Neva. Stella."

"No. I knew of them, of course, but I knew of you long before that."

"When?"

She twirled her yellow hair between her fingers. When you escaped to Earth with your parents."

"Ha! Now I had caught her. There was no way on this red planet Chandra could have known me as a baby when she was a baby at about the same time.

"You think I deceive you. Consider a life-span. How long do you think a monophylum can live do you suppose?"

"Let's see. A season," I'd guess. "If you were planted in the spring, grew to a ripe old age in the summer, and died in the fall, just before the snows came, that would mean you hadn't even lived a year."

"Shows how much you know," Chandra said, returning to the bed and sitting down. "You are right about the first part, of course. But when fall arrived, and I was ready to die, I didn't die as you can see. The day I met Neva and Stella, (Slew then), I had already discussed the likelihood of your existence for almost a millennium."

"Almost a thousand years? That's impossible!"

"Not impossible. Highly probable."

I smirked. "You sound just like Spock... You know Spock, from the Starship Enterprise."

"Oh, that. Those are fictional characters in case you forget."

I remembered. I also remembered the fantastic re-runs that Mom had actually let me watch. Much of my flat screen viewing had been limited to science programs and sorrowful sitcoms about real-life being replaced by mechanical wonders – and the news, of course. The officer who had found our car – the one with the one yellow eye, the mechanical cyborg – had once seemed fictional to me, until the day I saw him in living color, so perhaps Chandra had lived a thousand years.

"That's your name on the Iron Pillar," I said.

"Yes. It was created when I was born – when I became the Guardian."

"About that," I began, searching Chandra's green eyes for the truth. "You must be pretty smart."

"Smart enough to know why you're asking me that question."

"Well, if you're so smart, why don't you let me out of here, huh? You have to know that my father needs to be found."

"And why is that, Aaden?"

"Don't treat me like a two-year-old. Those, that Grude beast; his… *things* are taking over your planet."

"That's very astute of you."

"So, I'm not as stupid as you thought."

Chandra smiled. "I must go now," she said. "Give it time. When the stone glows like the color of my eyes, you will know I will return."

"And then what?"

Chandra stood and walked to the electronic door. "We will go in search of your father," she said.

Kathryn Elizabeth Jones

Grude

Chandra returned early the next morning. In-between that time, I'd seen Mom only twice, and she'd told me to keep busy making my wire animals. She'd brought my meals and pretty much forgotten all about me, at least that's how it seemed to me at the time.

When you're bored, and I was definitely that, your mind wanders and you imagine all sorts of things. Once, in mid-sleep, I thought Dad had returned, silver suit and all. He hung there on my ceiling and his voice sounded like Grude's.

"You will die," Dad said. "You will die and I will eat you."

Dad hung on my ceiling and continued to talk to me like a frenzied chimpanzee. Long before the Earth was destroyed, we no longer had zoos. Wild animals hadn't been kept behind bars for as long as I'd been a kid. After their ancestors, the ones my mom knew about when she was a little girl, had been trained to function in society, all wild animals after that had begun to be civilized by their parents. Like the plants, they were often misunderstood and undervalued, but this was because of people in general. Changing oneself was something grownups continued to have a problem with.

"Aaden, Aaden!" The voice seemed loud and quiet at the same time. And then I realized I was hearing it in my head. "The others, they are coming!"

I reached inside my pocket for the stone. It was glowing green! Grabbing the stuff that I had tucked at the side of my bed beforehand; I raced to the room and made my way through the wall. Triumph was nowhere in sight. Racing up the hall, I reached 'the room'. Walking through the wall, I entered. Barina stood at the console, but she was sleeping, her head lying limp on the flat screen.

"Now!" Chandra hollered into my ear.

In just that second, Neva entered. "Stop!" he hollered.

I pushed the appropriate buttons just in case the stone wasn't as powered up as I thought, looked down at the green stone in my hand, and blinked. The burning against my skin made my eyes water, and I seemed to burn forever before I suddenly felt solid rock beneath my feet again. Opening my eyes, I expected to see the red planet below me, dried plants, and no sign of water, but I hadn't transported myself to the same place.

I was staring into the red and piercing eyes of Grude himself!

"It was only a matter of time," he said.

I looked around me. I was underground as before; in the same room I'd slept in before lying my way out.

"The stone."

The green stone still glittered in my hand. I closed my fingers around it but could still see the green light shining through my skin.

"Now."

"No."

"Then, you will die, and we will have quite the meal here."

My heart stopped.

"Kill me then and take the stone."

The beast blinked, then howled loudly, shaking the walls. Any moment I thought the clear rock in which I was enclosed, would break, but it held fast.

"Give me the stone."

I held the stone tightly.

"Give him the stone," Chandra offered. I was amazed that she was in the room. I couldn't see her. Even more amazing that she'd told me to hand over the stone.

"No!" I shouted inside my head.

"It is the only way… to see your father."

I couldn't see Chandra anywhere, only Grude hovering nearby like a hairy bush.

"Where is he?"

After asking the question, it occurred to me that if Chandra was speaking into my mind, that Grude could also hear it. All of it.

"I wish to keep you safe."

"Then, speak aloud," I said.

A loud roar enveloped the room and in the next second a man was standing before me. "Father!"

I blinked once, twice, hoping that the vision would not end. It didn't. My dad said nothing. He didn't even reach for me. He wore the same silver suit, his eyes staring before him.

"Give Grude the stone." This time, the voice came into my natural ears and I saw Chandra. She stood next to my dad and was holding out her hand. No longer a girl, she'd reverted to her monophyla form. A tear had escaped her eye and her hand was trembling. "Please…" she uttered.

I don't know what made me do it. Maybe it was seeing my father for the first time in days. Maybe it was the tear or Chandra's monophyla hand reaching for me. But in that instant, before I had a chance to think about what I was doing, or what the motion might really mean, I had released the green stone into Chandra's waiting hand.

I ran to Dad. No-one stopped me. Not Grude. Not Chandra. Not the feeling I had that there were others in the room I could not see. My dad was warm but as stiff as a board. Hugging him was like I imagined it would feel embracing the Pillar of Delhi.

"What's wrong with him?" I asked, peering over at the beast.

"He is fossilized. Frozen in time."

"Why?"

"We needed him here when you arrived. The first time…" The beast stopped and looked over at Chandra. "He needed to be reminded."

Pulling myself from my father, I looked over at Chandra. "So, you're a part of this," I said.

"A part? Hardly."

"Stop!" The beast roared. "Take him to the chamber!"

An invisible hand suddenly reached for me, and as the glowing embers of the green stone filtered through the fingers of Chandra's hand, I was taken away by someone I could not see.

We were underground, I knew that, but the walls were glass like the ones in the room where I'd first slept. It was like they blinked at me as I walked with the invisible hand. And it seemed we walked forever. Nothing changed. Not the walls. Not the process of walking with the invisible being. And then, when I thought to have walked forever, we were at the end of the long, great tunnel.

It opened into a well-lit room, like the one I'd first entered when Chandra had teased me about Goldilocks and the Three Bears. In fact, it might have even been the same room. though there was no mush, no spoons on the table.

"Sit," she said, "and be quiet."

The monophylum revealed itself and took a chair opposite my own. For a brief moment, the eye stared into my soul. The thing that I'd never before met, wore no clothes, and at first, I wasn't even sure of its gender, but once it spoke, I felt I knew.

"What do you want from the green stone?" I asked.

"Want? Power, of course."

"Where is my father?"

"He is in safekeeping."

"Where?"

"Quiet. You must listen. The stone. Grude will do horrible things with the stone."

"Like read minds, go through walls? The beast can already do that."

"Silence!" She laid her forefinger against her thin lips. I realized then that she was a bit like Stella, though her skin wasn't as green, but had a faint tinge of yellow to it. "I – we are here to help you. Know that. No matter what ha –"

"Silence!" Grude hovered above me like a giant. "We will have silence! You are excused, Slew."

My thoughts drifted briefly to what I knew about that name; that it represented all of the monophyla race. But Grude was suddenly sitting on the chair opposite and looking with hatred into my eyes. He planted the stone on the table.

It was no longer green.

"I need this," he said. "Fix it."

I would have laughed if I hadn't been so scared. As it was, I knew how to fix it, but fixing it would take some time, time Grude would more than likely not want to wait for.

"What did you do to it?" I asked.

A large, hairy fist pounded the table. "Tell me!"

"You must have broken it."

"Tell me – now – or your father will die!"

Tears gathered in my eyes. I was no match for this beast and he knew it. "It takes time," I began. "How much time?"

"Twenty-four hours or so. It needs to recharge. Coming here took a lot of energy.

"I – A few hours, you say?"

I nodded, trying to avoid Grude's red eyes, but he was walking closer to me now, like a mechanical toy. It was strange, almost as if he was only half-beast. The thought had occurred to me before, upon first seeing him, and now it returned to haunt me. Was he some sort of Culem Borg, like the cop I'd met on Earth?

"You're right, of course," the beast said. "But I'm of a superior breed."

"What?"

"Your thoughts are not safe with me, and once the stone is re-activated, I will be the most powerful being on this planet and on any other."

I thought of the other planets nearby. Only three of them were habitable, I remembered, and we were on one of them. That meant there were yet two planets near the red star, planets Grude wanted to rule over as well as this one. He'd somehow managed the take-over with the monophyla, and now he wanted more. Power was like that.

My thoughts drifted briefly to the power I'd once sought, and I felt ashamed.

Grude smiled smugly at me.

"All you humans are alike. You have this – what shall I call it – a sense of fair play. A desire to do the right thing, to be good and kind. I don't understand it."

I knew what the beast was getting at, and I also knew that I wasn't going to share what I knew with him. If he pried it from my brain, fine, but I would never voluntarily share anything I didn't want to.

"That's fine, too." Grude reached for the stone, and, placing it in a bag he wore around his waist, stood to leave.

"So, you are no longer afraid of the stone?" I asked. "Is it because the stone is dark?"

"It is amazing how close you think like the monophyla here. Like you, they were an easy race to conquer," Grude said, not answering either question.

He shuffled stiffly to the entrance and left me. When I could no longer see him up the tunnel I spoke to Chandra. But she didn't reply. I reached through my thoughts to my father but felt nothing from him either. It was hours later that I realized I'd reached out without the aid of the stone.

Somehow, the man (or beast) handling of the stone made sense to me. Chandra had taken it from my hand – she was pure. Grude, in all of his stumbling wickedness, could not.

I must have been deep in sleep when I heard Chandra speak to me. I flicked my eyes open. The room was still lit by some un-earthly source that penetrated the walls. But I couldn't see Chandra anywhere.

Fortunately, I'd been given a covering that somewhat resembled a blanket, though the material felt more like plastic, and reminded me of one of those blankets one packed for emergencies – the thin silver kind.

I blinked again, listening.

"We don't have much time," Chandra said. "Make your way through the walls."

"Why should I?" I spurted. "You – you brought me here, made me give the stone to Grude. I don't trust you!"

"What?"

"Where are you taking me now, to my death? Is it time for the next meal?"

"Listen. Make your way through the walls."

"You're crazy. I'm staying right here!"

There was silence, unbreathable silence as I waited for Chandra's reply. When none came, I asked: "Why did you do it?"

"I had to. All of the monophyla here are under the strict control of Grude. You have to know I didn't want to bring you back here."

"How do I know you're telling me the truth?" I asked.

"You don't, I guess unless you'd like to trust your heart."

A part of me did; still, I was mad. My dad wasn't even the same, and now Chandra was asking me to move through the walls without the stone?

Still, I could hear her even now, and I no longer had the stone.

"Are you listening?"

I nodded as if Chandra could see me. And maybe she could.

Standing from the bed, I dropped the silver blanket and walked to the walls. I was angry at her for taking the green stone, but something about her actions prevented me from speaking the same aloud.

Reaching my hand to the glass, I touched, for the very first time, the sleekness and coldness of it.

You know how it feels when you first leave the house during the winter, and the icy wind hits your face? Well, that's how it felt when I left the room through the glass wall.

My fingers were suddenly traveling to the other side, and then I was taking my body beyond my glass prison. Stepping through the wall this time wasn't a bit like the first time, though the result was the same. I was on the other side, but it was terribly cold. Wrapping my hands around my bare arms I proceeded forward, for there was suddenly a path before me.

"This must be the yellow brick road," I said in my mind, thinking of The Wizard of Oz, one of the movies my mother watched every year before Christmas. As I told you before, she liked the old classics, and I guess forcing me to watch them had sort of warmed my heart to them too. But now I was very cold.

"You need to be silent. Just follow the path. Try to clear your mind of any and all thoughts. Grude or one of his minions will find you if you don't."

She was right, of course. It had happened before, and it would surely happen again if I wasn't careful. But it was hard to clear my mind of anything; I wasn't a spiritual guru after all, and thoughts had a tendency to run through my mind like a hovercar.

I thought I was doing a fair job of it, though, until Chandra stood before me, yellow hair and all. "Shhh!" she said, placing her finger over my lips. "We are almost there."

I almost asked, 'Where?' but we were suddenly looking into a room. Inside was my father. He appeared to be asleep. He was still wearing his torn silver suit. He faced the glass wall, his blanket tucked tightly over his shoulders.

I watched as Chandra touched him on the arm. And then, in moments that seemed like hours, he sat up and looked into my eyes.

There was recognition there, but something else, something that scared me almost as much as Grude finding us out and walking into the room.

My father smiled. "You," he said.

Chandra placed a thin finger over his lips and directed him to me. "Grude will not sleep long," she said, taking my father by the hand. "Follow me."

I didn't ask why she had to hold my father's hand, and why she didn't take mine. Not that I wanted her to take it, the movement was just funny, that's all. I followed the two of them out the entrance and up the tunnel. In time we'd reached the same place that would lead us to the surface.

But there was something foul in the pit of my stomach, so foul I almost let what was in my stomach spill to the floor of the cavern.

"You can do it," Chandra said. "The stone, it is only a means…"

A loud thud entered the chamber. I didn't have to look to know who was there. Closing my eyes, I thought of being above the surface with my father and Chandra.

"You think to escape me!" the voice roared.

I tried to clear my mind of everything but what it would mean to leave this place and return to the home

I'd known for five years. Taking a deep breath, I waited. A furry paw touched my bare arm, and as I was about to recoil, something incredible happened.

We emerged.

On the surface, Chandra screamed, "Run!"

I didn't look back. Taking my father's hand, we ran together, as some sort of threesome, over the red dirt, the rocks, and dead plant life. The air was hot, almost smoldering, but still, we ran. I didn't look back once, and the furry paw that I'd felt just seconds prior did not reach for me.

We had run some distance when I gasped for breath.

"We cannot stop!" Chandra roared. "There! See that?"

Suddenly, I tripped.

When I looked up, Mom was standing above me. Her face and arms were splotched a muted red, and her hair was shorter than I remembered it. There was a strange smell, like something burning.

"So, you thought to sneak out again!" she hollered, blinking down at me. Yes, even her eyelids looked burned. "Well, at least you did one thing right."

I supposed she was referring to saving dad. But where had she *come from*?

"It's good to see you again, too," Mom said, reaching for my dad's hand and kissing him softly on the lips. I almost gagged.

I looked around me. Neva was suddenly there, and Stella.

"You didn't really think I'd let you escape from me twice," Mom said.

Standing, I looked around me. "I don't see Grude anywhere."

"There." Stella pointed one long green finger in the direction of the Pillar of Delhi. But I couldn't see anything but the pillar. We were too far from it.

"Grude has power, but not all power," Neva said. "Still…" He looked around as if he was suddenly afraid of something. "The stone will soon regain its power, and then he will come in search of you."

I was suddenly shaking my head. I don't know when it had occurred to me that Grude would never be able to use the stone without my help, but the thought was suddenly there, swirling inside my brain. "I thought you had to have faith to use the stone," I said to no one in particular. "You can't go on some sort of power trip to make it work. Does the stone also have to be for others, and not specifically for yourself?"

Dad nodded. "There are others underground with the goodness and faith to use it that is if Grude gets desperate enough and goes to them for help."

"What is it that he wants?" I asked.

Mom placed her arm around me. "I'm so glad you're safe," she said.

I was glad I was safe too, but she hadn't answered my question.

Stella took my hand. "You will know in time," she said. "Right now, it's important that we get you back to the plane."

Without the stone – it was still in Grude's hairy hands – I was at a loss as to how this was going to happen. But then I remembered. The others, they had come without it.

"I'm sorry," I said.

Dad placed his hand around my back, and along with Mom, we waited for the moment the plane would return to us.

Only it didn't happen.

We sat for nearly an hour of Earth time, and I could tell Chandra was getting nervous. Finally, she said, "So, what's up? I thought you had things worked out."

I funneled the red sand between my fingers and tried not to whine. "I'm hungry."

"We're all hungry." Neva planted himself on my shoulders. "It should have happened by now."

Mom nodded. "When I was sent down, I was told they would be right behind me, wanting to keep the plane safe and away from prying eyes until the last millisecond." Mom hesitated briefly and continued: "Barina warned us when I came down, that things might not go as smoothly as I wanted them to, that we didn't have a very long stay above ground before death."

"Is that why your skin is so red?" I asked.

Mom nodded.

69

"Barina told us not to come, but how could I leave you and your father here?"

"Now, we're all trapped," I said.

"Maybe not," Dad said standing. "Where would they have landed the space plane?"

"So, it's crash-landed?"

Stella shrugged, but Neva hopped off of my shoulder. "I hear them now," she said. "The plane is just over that rise!"

I looked where Neva's forefinger pointed and saw nothing but red dirt and a small hill. But I did see something in the distance the opposite way. The image was coming toward us, and it was getting nearer each moment we spoke.

"What do you think it is?" I asked.

"Better to cloak ourselves rather than find out too late," Neva answered.

Without another thought, I made the change. The ground shook beneath me, and as I watched the thing pace the area, I was almost sure it could smell us.

Moments later, however, the beast stormed past us and returned in the direction he had come.

"I know what you're thinking, Aaden," Neva said. "But many of these beasts do not hold yet hold the same powers that Grude does. Did you notice that the beast walked to us firmly, without hesitation?"

Actually, I hadn't. I had just wanted the thing gone.

"He is of the first breed."

"The first breed?" Mom asked.

"Not yet taken over by cyborg parts."

I thought again of the police cyborg, and then about the mechanical walk of Grude. "You mean these bear beasts are being transformed?"

"Yes," Dad said. "And there may be more where we are going. They may have already discovered the spaceplane."

Kathryn Elizabeth Jones

Bear Beasts

It occurred to me days later that the bear beasts actually had a breed name, but at that moment, looking over the rise and seeing a group of them huddled around the space plane, I couldn't think about anything but death.

They had more than likely killed Barina, and even Triumph, though my traveling companions might have made themselves invisible before the horrible act. I could only imagine what the beasts ate, though I'd already been threatened to be eaten by Grude.

"Our friends' powers are dimming," Stella said.

Neva nodded. "We need to release them from the plane before they reveal themselves."

In our current situation, I figured the feat would be easy, but I quickly learned the truth. "We have very little power left ourselves. Aaden, you must help us."

My heart pounded in unbelief. "Me?"

"You are the only one."

"In case you forgot…"

"You don't need the stone," Mom said.

It was the craziest thing I'd ever heard. And yet, hadn't I gotten everyone above ground just hours before? And hadn't I just made everyone invisible when the bear beast had walked by?

Dad nodded his head as if he somehow understood, and Mom agreed. "It has always been possible," she said.

I cleared my mind of any and all things and thought of faith moving us toward our goal without being seen. It was crazy, but I was starting to believe it. Today was a grand day. I would be able to show others of my powers. I would be able to save myself and everyone else!

"Aaden!"

"What?" I blubbered.

Suddenly, one of the bear beasts stood in front of me. In a blink, we were invisible again, but it was like I could see my feet and then I couldn't, like a blinking light that was going on and off. "What do I do?" I screamed inside my head, knowing the monophyla could hear my thoughts as well as possibly some of the bear beasts.

"You must be quick to think of others – only others."

I would be lying to you if I said that, at that moment, I listened, but my mind was suddenly muddied up, and I was thinking of how we were all going to die if I didn't do this thing right. I blinked over at the hairy beasts as we arrived and were hidden from their view and arrived once more. And before I knew it, the beasts, all six of them, held us roughly by the arms.

I could smell the stench of decaying fruit even before the largest of them spoke.

"I knew you would be found in time," it said.

"Where are my friends?" I asked.

"So, those two plants are friends of yours?" He bored his red, hateful eyes in the direction of Neva, Stella, and Chandra. "The slew have always been a weak race, no matter their form," he said.

I looked briefly at Chandra, who had at one time or another returned to her monophyla form.

"I knew we couldn't trust you," the beast said. "Come with us!"

I turned from the space plane, still searching in my mind for the voices of Triumph and Barina. But there was nothing but silence. Were they dead within the space plane, crumpled in heaps and half-eaten? I hadn't liked Triumph, at least not much, but Barina had tried to be my friend.

Walking through the heated red sands, I thought of my temper as well as my pride. Minutes, that seemed like hours later, we'd returned to the Iron Pillar of Delhi, held securely by the beasts.

I was the worst person ever born. Could a good person hate anyone, even if someone or some 'thing' treated them cruelly or used them for their own selfish purposes? Could a good person think only of himself especially in the worst possible moment?

Do you know how you hope for things that never happen? You know, like a new toy you've always wanted, but never got? Considering that wanting to escape was even more important than a toy, you'd think my powers would work, but they didn't. As the pillar overshadowed us and the door opened, I could only blink back the tears and walk forward as the head beast pushed me inside.

I thought of my dad. He was pretty strong, I knew that, but he was obviously no match for the beasts that held us now. Back through the tunnels we went, smelling that constantly decaying smell, and wondering what was going to happen next.

When we reached the room, the same room I could have explained by now with my eyes shut, I was pushed inside with the others, and we all stood and huddled together near the glass walls.

Grude was suddenly at the entrance.

"So, you decided to escape your fate."

He walked inside, holding the green stone that wasn't green. And I knew why, just as I knew why I hadn't been able to make my parents and friends invisible. It was all about selfishness, wasn't it? All about power, though not the kind of power that was good and wise, but the controlling stuff.

"I thought to wield this stone to my desires, but it did not return to all of its glory," he said, placing the stone on the table with a growl. The thing was as dark as my soul felt. "Fix it!" he snarled, pounding the table and making the stone jump.

I could feel my parents to my left and my monophyla friends to my right, but they said nothing.

I had no idea what to do. I couldn't make my friends invisible, and I couldn't make the stone work.

"I can feel your thoughts, but you are trying to trick me," the beast said. "Chandra, the Guardian..." He smirked once and continued, "...may have gotten you to the surface without the stone, but I know your power with it. With the stone, you can walk through walls, hear the conversation inside the heads of all, and even transport yourself from a plane to the ground. So, you can help me!"

He roared again and, walking to the table, I reached for the stone.

It lit up when I touched it, a glowing green.

"Just as I predicted!" the beast sang.

I couldn't believe it; the stone was shining. So, it had been given enough time to recharge, though the beast hadn't been able to activate it.

"Who are you anyway?" I asked, the stone glowing within my hand. "What do you want from this stone?"

The beast stomped closer to me, and reaching for the stone, pulled back. "Hand it to me," he ordered.

"Are you sure?" I asked.

The beast grew angry. "Now!"

Suddenly, as the stone reached Grude's fingertips, lightning filled the room. Green sparks sprayed from the surface of the stone and lit up the room like the 4th of July.

Grude yelled, and dropping the stone, thumped to the entrance where he stood, gasping for air, holding his burned paw close to his body.

The stone still glowed, but just barely, and I knew what would come next.

"Pick up the stone!" Grude barked.

Chandra walked forward, her small feet tapping the floor. She picked up the stone. It lit briefly, and just as suddenly, darkened. She reached for Grude.

I tried not to smile as the beast recoiled, thoughts of getting burned again obvious in his red eyes. But he wouldn't be burned, not now – now that the stone was dark.

"I will just have to make good use of you in the future," he said, taking the stone in the next second within his unharmed paw. "The others, well, I have no need of them. They will die at my earliest convenience."

I held my mother and father close after that. Neva and Stella stood nearby, huddled together as if sharing their last words, for surely, they must have been sharing something like that though I didn't hear them. This was their last moment together, just like it was the last moment for me and my parents.

I had lost them and found them only to lose them again.

I wiped my eyes but the tears kept coming.

"You can do this," Mom said. "You don't need the stone."

I didn't believe her. But I had to know something. "What does the stone do?" I asked.

Stella was suddenly beside me. She hopped onto my shoulder, the place where Neva usually found himself. She stroked my face. "Your mother is right. You *can* do this."

"No, I can't."

"You have lived in error, but we all have done the same."

"I have lived in so much error that I'm finished with it all."

"That is an untruth. Consider how far you have come – how far *we* have come. Without you, we would have been lost."

"You can't mean that," I sniffed. "I am nothing. I don't deserve to live."

You may not believe me, but in that exact moment, I truly believed the words I spoke. I had ruined everything. I hadn't even managed to get us above ground to safety, after all, Chandra had done that. I wasn't good for anything.

"I heard that," Chandra said, taking my hand. She was a girl again, a beautiful girl with yellow hair and piercing green eyes. I could have loved her if I hadn't known the truth.

"I'm not going to help Grude. I will die with you."

"We can yet escape through the walls," Neva said, hopping on my other shoulder.

"Yes, with Chandra's help."

Chandra smiled up at me. "Let Grude think what he wants. I didn't bring us to the surface."

"But, aren't you the Guardian?" I asked weakly.

"I used to protect the clan," Chandra said, releasing my hand. Her purple train moved across the floor as she paced in front of us. "I used to have the power. Like you, it began with the stone, but when the stone was taken from me and to Earth by the Ursus, the power within me dimmed until it was no more."

"The Ursus?"

"The one you know as Grude and his followers. We have all been held captive. This is our world, and after Earth was destroyed, the Ursus needed another place to live."

"What?" I gasped.

"This is a lot to take in, but you must know of it now before it's too late. I feel there is not much time."

"The Ursus have lived on your planet for millennia. When they learned that Earth would be destroyed, and finding no way to prevent it, their place of residence was suddenly in jeopardy. They had to find another place to live. *We* were the other."

A creepy feeling entered my heart then, so creepy that I'm not even sure I can tell you about it. But I need to tell you about it. And I need to tell you now.

The bear we saw, the one from Earth at the time of the apocalypse, that bear was one of them. No wonder he wasn't dead. No wonder he was there walking the mountains as if nothing had happened.

"Was it Grude?" I asked, for even though Chandra had lost most of her power, something yet remained, the ability to read minds.

"Yes."

Still, I couldn't remember that bear walking mechanically like he was part cyborg, but maybe…

"You're right. The transformation was only forming during the Earth's destruction. We learned later that Grude almost died."

"How did he make it off of Earth? Did he have a space plane?" I asked.

Tears suddenly gathered in Chandra's eyes. "You won't believe it," she said.

"I will believe it," I countered, looking into her eyes.

"He and some of the others traveled with Neva's master."

"What?"

Suddenly the room was full of the Ursus breed, and they were glaring at us. "No more talk!" Grude shouted, pulling Chandra by the arm. "She will die first!"

Chandra was silent as Grude dragged her from the room.

"What do they eat?" I had the courage to ask.

Dad looked into my eyes. "Everything," he said.

Revival

I had been given many chores when we lived on Earth, from cleaning the car port to emptying the dish blower, but this task was beyond anything I would have considered then.

I had to save the life of Chandra.

My mom and dad stood on either side of me, Neva and Stella still on my shoulders. We were all silent, but I could feel the air as if it could speak. This was the time. Either I would be afraid for the rest of my life, or I would finally and completely rely on the power of the stone.

And yet, perhaps this is what Chandra and the others had wanted me to learn. I could do it – somehow – without the stone. But how?

Looking inside my brain, I remembered the times the stone had helped me. I'd found it in the cave, I'd used it to escape from this very prison, I'd even used it to come to the surface of the red star. How could I do anything without it? But Chandra had said that it wasn't she who had placed them on the surface the last time. Though Grude had somehow thought it had to have been her, the power hadn't come from Chandra, but from me.

How was that possible?

I shivered, though I wasn't cold, and thought of Chandra being led to her death. I could actually see her through the walls, and beyond the long hall that joined another chamber. They were all there. Chandra, Grude and about fifty of the Ursus breed. The room was lit up, the walls like glass. The stone, still black, was tightened within Grude's paw.

He held it high. "The first!" he shouted.

Chandra was once more monophylum. She stood, erect, her small form as straight as a corn stalk taking in the nourishment of the sun. The others glowered near her, saliva escaping their lips. So, she would be eaten.

At that moment, it was all about Chandra. I closed my eyes and breathed into the air. Suddenly, the room was damp as if it had just rained, and I was sailing through the walls as if on an ancient ship cruising the waters. In a blink, maybe less, I had reached her.

Holding her within my arms I was feeling successful when a hairy paw reached out.

"Enough!" the beast shouted, pulling me from the wall.

I opened my eyes. Chandra lay at my feet.

"I may not have the powers of this stone." He held the black rock in front of him. "But there are other powers yet to escape me!"

Shoving me to the ground, I was bound to Chandra.

"In time the stone will glow again and you will show me how to use it!"

I couldn't believe it, any of it. "You will never be able to use the green stone!" I yelled before thinking.

I heavy slap reached my lip. Blood dripped to the floor.

"Son!"

Mom's voice did little to soothe me, neither did my father's thoughts of bravery. I could feel them all. The fear of my monophyla friends, and the heavy beating of my heart.

The task would not be easy if not impossible. I'm not sure how many days we spent held captive, but it was long enough to know how hungry really felt. Most of the time I slept. Without the stone, and without the power to do anything but sit, I was left alone.

The others shared a similar fate, and while in the same room as myself, we spoke little. It was if they'd also realized their ultimate fate. It wouldn't do them any good to scream, to try to rid themselves of the clamps around their own wrists and ankles.

Mom cried mostly, along with Stella. In-between the crying, Neva would try to get me to do something, and my dad would follow his lead with unpleasant encouragement of his own. *Wriggle your hands. Think of breaking the bonds. Can you remove them at your feet?* I didn't want to listen to any of it.

Finally, when hope was all but gone, Chandra said something that made me turn, however slightly, to her. The hold between us was tight, but I could still feel her pressed against my back, smell her breath, and imagine to myself what she must truly be thinking about me.

"We will be eaten soon," she said. "The Ursus don't eat daily, but weekly forage for the food they need."

"Great," I answered, dreading my language as quickly as it escaped my lips. Or, was I only thinking it?

"Our love cannot die here," she said. "Remember, I am here to help you always."

I almost responded with another snarky remark about her hair but refrained. *Our love?* Had she really said, *Our love?*

"Listen..."

"I'm tired of listening!"

"Your father is right. You can break the bonds that hold all of us."

"No, I can't."

"The time is nearing."

"I want to be eaten. I'm sick of sitting here."

I wasn't at first sure if Chandra had heard me, and then I heard sobbing. "You're...you're a creep, do you know that?"

I almost laughed. If I hadn't been so hungry and sick of it all, I would have.

"Where did you learn that word?" I asked.

"I didn't say anything," Chandra whispered.

"Mom?"

"I know you don't want to hear it, but you can get us out of here."

"Why did you call me a creep?"

"It was the only way to get you to listen to me."

"I'm sorry, Mom. I can't do it."

"You'll do it, Son. And right now, if you know what's good for you."

I hated them... hated them all.

"We know you can do it." Was that Neva?

"Listen, we all know you have the power to do it." Stella?

"Shut up!" I said.

The place was suddenly lit up by a hairy beast. Well, he'd probably heard the entire conversation. It was too late now. "Can't you see I'm trying to sleep?" he boomed, hovering above me. Saliva from its hairy mouth dripped directly onto my head. I could feel the terrible disgusting slime travel down one side of my face.

"Sorry. I didn't mean it."

"Sorry? You, humans, are so weak!"

"Whatever you say," I mumbled, staring at the feet of the beast who was obviously guarding us.

The thing laughed, stomping its foot and making the glass walls shake. "Not much longer, and we can eat," it said, still standing before me like a hairy pillar.

I spit, but nothing came out. So, I was dehydrated too. We'd had a little water – or something that had resembled it, since being captured. We'd even had a taste or two of some runny mush, but nothing more.

"Eat me now," I ventured, knowing that once the words were out, there was no going back.

"What did you say?"

"He said, to eat him." Was that Chandra speaking?

"I just might." The beast lifted me with one arm, undid the chain with one paw holding me to the wall, and pulled me to his eyes. They were red and glaring just like the beast I knew and hated so well. The beast walked me to the corner of the room where some sort of ancient table stood. I'd never seen it before. But it looked old, the surface like a gnarled tree from Earth which had been made for such a sacrifice as myself. I fit on it perfectly.

The breath of the beast bore down on me and I almost threw up what little food I had. Instead of focusing on my stomach, however, I had an immediate thought that surrounded me so fully, I wondered if I'd actually thought it.

"He isn't changed..."

In an instant, it occurred to me that the beast hadn't yet been modified. He wasn't yet cyborg. I hadn't heard or felt a halt in its step.

"What do I do?"

"I am ready."

Do you know how you know something without really knowing that you know it? You feel you have been somewhere before or know someone, I mean, really know them, when in fact you've just met? Well, this is how I felt at that moment. I knew what I had to do as if I'd already lived this moment and the people, plants, and beasts within it.

I reached out. I was already on the table, and the beast was so close to me, I could see the fine hairs around its eyes. Its mouth opened, revealing white teeth and a foul smell. I almost heaved.

In the briefest of seconds, perhaps one or two breaths, the clasps on my ankles fell followed by those on my wrists. Those on my ankles clanked to the floor.

The beast plunged his fist into my chest. I was momentarily stunned.

"Not yet!" he howled, pulling my left arm to its mouth.

And in just that second, I was gone.

I felt the dampness of the room as in days before. And in my mind's eye, I could see the green stone in another room, sitting alone on an equally crude end table, Grude asleep.

Smiling, I spoke to the others silently, demanding that they follow me to the surface of the planet. The portal, the one we had used before, was no longer necessary. The air was hot, and like before, we had to move quickly. I had no time to think about what had just happened, how I'd managed to extricate myself and everyone I loved from that room. We were suddenly above ground and at the spaceplane.

Once there, Dad checked for damage. It was like a huge puzzle lay before him and all of his thoughts were occupied in completing it. The outward hull was damaged, one of its four wings bent and sagging. The beasts had lodged their paws within the door. Gaping holes showed the bareness of the plane's interior. I could not see Barina and Triumph, neither could I feel them.

Walking inside, I halted. No, there was no one here. The console was still intact, but I couldn't get the plane to start. The engine didn't even groan.

I turned to my dad. He looked at me, fear revealing his true thoughts. Mom held Stella's hand, and together they watched as Neva worked on the greatest damage. But it was no use. The plane wouldn't start.

Freedom?

It came to me that the beasts had been able to bend and tear the plane with their bare claws when I'd previously deemed the task impossible. After all, the iron that fitted the plane together was the same metal as my flashlight – the one I held in my backpack – and the same metal of the Iron Pillar of Delhi.

When it occurred to me that the only thing that could fix the plane was a miracle, I thought of faith, and then I thought of the green stone. It was not with me, but it might still be able to help us.

I touched the ragged surface of the plane with my hand. The sudden jolt of metal smoothing out and the clicking of gears, made me jump, along with everyone else I loved. As the plane shook, and everyone sat but me, I reached for the console. With just a touch, the console righted itself and began to purr.

"Way to go, Son!" Mom cheered.

Dad was quickly by my side, directing me.

I couldn't believe it, any of it, but then I could. My hands were once again on the drive console and Dad continued to instruct me until the plane leveled out. Later, when things got quieter, Neva spoke to me sternly about my clogged ears, as I had purposely not listened to my dad when I needed to. But now the plane was in opt drive and I could get some rest as Dad watched the console for a few hours.

But it was hard to sleep. All I could think about was how I'd saved everyone, and that I had some strange power that went even further than the power of the green stone.

What did that make me?

When my eyes blinked open a couple of hours later, and I realized I'd finally found sleep, I found my mom and dad in 'the room' along with Neva and Stella. As promised, they were waiting for me.

"Did you sleep?" I asked, taking the plane out of opt-drive and placing my hands on the drive console "Wow. Where are we?" I asked.

"It's called Spectra." Stella's voice was as light as a feather and as penetrating as the glass is to skin. "It is the homeworld."

I looked beyond me to the skies. "Sorry," I managed, "but shouldn't we leave here and find another place to live?"

Someone gasped from behind me. "You can't leave them," Stella said, reaching me and hopping on my shoulder. Neva followed. I could feel them both there, like angels' wings.

"Why not?" I asked, for even then, after everything, I often still thought of myself.

"There are others of our kind," Neva said, placing his thin fingers on my neck. "They must be saved."

"How many?" I asked.

"Hundreds," Chandra answered, walking up to

"Wait! You weren't trying to take over the planet, too were you?"

Neva breathed into my ear. "At first," she admitted. "The Ursus convinced us of your terror. They found you first, altered their genetics as part of evolution, extended their life through your technology, and brought us in when we could no longer live on the surface of Spectra – and the other planets."

I couldn't believe it! "You came to take over Earth?"

"It was the plan... at first."

"Neva, who *was* your master?" I asked.

Neva brushed his thin fingers against my skin. "I suppose I can tell you now," he said.

Kathryn Elizabeth Jones

The Master's Aid

I don't think Neva was too proud of what he told me next – I wouldn't be – but then again, the truth was always better than falsehood, and I was determined to learn all I could to become the leader everyone seemed to expect me to be.

"He was Ursus," Neva began.

Somehow, I wasn't surprised. I waited for Neva to continue.

"He'd taken me against my will to Earth. I was his slave as he studied the humans."

"And the day you found me?" I asked, turning my head back to the console.

"Master Lorm was dead."

"From what?"

Neva moved strangely on my shoulder. "Human sickness."

"What kind of human sickness? Did you kill him?"

The remark was rude, but there was something about Neva's hesitation in telling me the truth that had piqued my interest.

The monophylum was silent, and so was everyone else in the room.

"Well?"

Neva jumped from my shoulder. Peering up at me from the base of the console, he reached his thin, green arms consolingly in front of him. And then he did something even stranger.

"Master," he began, his slight head bowed so I could no longer see his green eye. "Master, you must forgive me. I have sworn with an oath not to lie."

Placing the plane in opt drive, I lifted the monophylum to his feet. Taking him in my arms I looked into his face. His green eye blinked at me, and suddenly, a tear escaped.

"Did you kill your master?" I asked.

If I could really tell you how I felt at that moment, you would think me something grand, but then, so long ago, all I could think about was Neva. He had been my friend since the beginning. When my parents couldn't be found, he'd been there. During every problem within the caves and on planet Earth before we had finally and forever left it, he had been there to help me. On the space plane, he hadn't given up on me, even when I no longer spoke to him.

"Yesssss," Neva answered. "I killed him."

I stroked Neva's face. "It's alright," I said. But someone nearby was gasping, and I could feel their rising anger. Chandra?

"You will die for your insolence!" she commanded.

Her words made me jump. I turned to face her, Neva still within my arms.

Stella jumped from my shoulder and ran to Chandra, her small feet padding across the glossy surface of the plane.

"I don't believe it! I don't believe – you!"

"I am the Guardian. Rules must be obeyed. A lie is not acceptable. A death claims death."

I couldn't see Stella's eye, but I could feel her anger rising. "At a time like this, when we are set and ready to bring back our families, you think to take a life because of a broken rule? Weren't we all coming down to murder the humans? Weren't we all going to take their Earth for ourselves? What does that make *us*?"

"You recall, Stella that we didn't kill the humans, didn't have to kill the humans. We didn't have to break our vow!"

"But we would have, had not their two nearby planets done the deed for us!"

Chandra was silent. Her green lips, for she'd suddenly turned from her human to her monophyla form, opened in silence. She said nothing, only stared over at her compatriot.

"There is a difference here!"

I looked briefly at my mom and dad, hoping they had something to say. They didn't but stood rigidly in the same place they'd been standing when I'd entered the room.

"We cannot kill our own kind," the Guardian said.

Stella kneeled. Bowing before the Guardian, she spoke softly. "The Ursus is not of our own kind."

Something happened to Chandra's skin then. Like a vast emptiness had grown behind her pores, her eye grew dull and her skin changed from green to yellow. I had seen this before, with Neva and Slew (before she became Stella). White would come next, and then death.

"They have owned us for an eternity," Stella began." Once we were discovered by them, they lied, telling us that we could live with them in peace if we assisted them in the vanquishing of the humans. And so, we assisted them, becoming their slaves in the process. And now, now that the Earth is gone, we are still their slaves, and will be forevermore unless we kill them all!"

I was up to speed on this heated conversation until the last few words. It was then I wondered if my heart had stopped beating and if I hadn't awoken from my sleep at all. But in the next moment, I knew the truth.

Chandra lunged for Stella and took her to the ground. I couldn't believe what I saw. Neva jumped from my arms and managed his way in-between them. With his thin arms and nimble fingers, he pulled them apart. They collapsed in a heap at his feet.

"Enough! Enough, I tell you! I did what was necessary for the survival of the chosen one!"

It was then I managed to blink. I stared at Neva, and as he turned to me, I saw a power in his eye I had never seen before. "I saved the chosen one!"

I don't know if I can tell you how I felt then, but it was like a glow entered my feet and ran through my organs and through the top of my head. I knew Neva spoke the truth. He had saved me from his Master.

Learning that Neva had saved me from death, softened my soul in ways hard to explain. So, the man had discovered my identity, and Neva had saved me from certain death through the administering of poison.

I had learned all about poisonous plants found in the mountains in school, and so it didn't seem strange to me that Neva also knew of plants, the good as well as the evil ones. He was an advanced plant after all.

I'd never met the death camas, even in their less than advanced form, and never wanted to. But, evidently, Neva had, and he had known just what to do to get rid of his cruel master. And for that, I was grateful.

Hours later, when emotions had calmed, and we could speak to each other – without yelling – we were able to work out a plan on how to save the monophyla on Spectra without harming the Ursus breed.

The plan would be difficult.

Though Spectra was the governing planet, two others, smaller in size, yet held those unaffiliated in the running of the planets. The young and aged lived below ground on these two worlds and would live there forever until a suitable place could be found. There were millions of monophyla that had been forced to travel underground for safety when their star remained hot and they could no longer survive above ground.

Unfortunately, this truth had been purposeful for the Ursus who had found them. Having transformed to live on practically any surface of the land, they had been able to convince the monophyla that life on Earth would be preferable to returning to the Rentaurus System where their species had first developed.

But again, the plan to save them would be difficult.

If I'd been sure of my powers then, I was even less sure of my powers after the plan was initiated. I hadn't yet been told of the real power held within the stone, the power that Grude obviously didn't have, but wanted. And I wasn't so sure trying to save the monophyla without this knowledge was going to help me. I'd tried and failed numerous times to extricate the information from anyone left on board, with no results. And when it finally came time to put our thoughts into action, I would be lying to you if I said I wasn't afraid.

I wasn't even sure if the plan would work.

Kathryn Elizabeth Jones

Blast from the Past

You may not believe me when I tell you what happened next. But then again, if you've been with me this far, you know it takes a lot for me to give up on my plans.

Minutes after our conversation about saving the monophyla, and hiding our plane behind tall, thick brush-like tumbleweed, we'd made our way to the second of the three planets. As before, we located the Pillar of Delhi and made our way invisibly below.

The planet must have been apprised of our escape from Spectra because there were many Ursus guarding the children in their underground habitations. I didn't see any old, and realized, for the first time, that they must be inhabiting the third planet in this system.

"It will not be long," Chandra began, taking my hand in our invisibility. "You must take them now. You are close enough to take them with your powers."

I closed my eyes, ready for the transport to the surface. There were many of them, near 2,000. I could feel them – all of them.

"Now!" Chandra whispered.

But something was suddenly – wrong. The smell…

Rough hands found my arms, and in seconds, everyone who had come with me was revealed.

The largest of the Ursus stepped forward. The beast held pride in its eyes taller than a mountain. It, too, had red eyes and pointed teeth, but unlike Grude, its face was thinner, and its limbs, leaner.

"So, you thought to wield the power of the stone?" the beast said, smiling.

The beast wore a wicked smile like it was angry and happy at the same time.

"I am Presda," it said. "And you are my prisoners."

Chandra released my hand. "We have come for the young ones," she said, stepping forward boldly.

"Is that really you?"

Chandra was in her human form, her hair spilling over her shoulders like golden rain. She was beautiful in that moment, as beautiful as I'd ever seen her.

"It's me."

"Unbelievable that you prefer the human form to that of the other."

Chandra blushed. "You have no idea what I prefer," she said.

The beast moved forward. This time I noticed the mechanical steps. It reached forth its furry hand and lifted Chandra by the neck.

At that moment, that everlastingly long moment, I knew what I needed to do. "Stop!" I wailed, reaching for the beast's arm, and yanking it by the hair.

A strength I did not know I had forced the beast to release its tight grip. Chandra tumbled to the ground in monophyla form. Gasping for breath, she looked up at her captor, her green eye blinking in hate.

I heard my father's voice, my mother's cry as a slap found my face, sending me to the opposite wall. Next to the glass, I tried to move my right arm, but it fell loose at my side. I couldn't sit up. Neva was on my shoulder. I couldn't see Stella.

"So, you think to defeat me! The one true Ursus! But I will show you how I easily wield my power!"

"You sound just like Grude," I managed to mumble, still lying on the floor.

"Grude? You dare to defile me with that name?"

"You know him then?"

"Know him? We – "

A sudden shock of knowledge traveled through my feet and to my head. This beast had to be a woman, and the beast called Grude, he must have been her husband or companion, or something. I would have laughed if I hadn't felt so broken.

"And now," the beast continued, "we are separate. I have the best part of the deal, shaping innocent minds to my liking, while he... he spends his time thinking of ways to gain more power from the stone. Has he done so?" she asked.

"Not yet," I mumbled again.

"And he may never discover it," she said. "But you know it, don't you, human?"

It seemed the beast searched my mind then and came away empty, for suddenly, she stomped her foot and turned from me. "Bring them to the chamber," she said.

Do you know how your room smells when you've forgotten to clean it? Laundry is the worst. One day my mom came to me. She said, "Aaden, you are now in charge of washing your own clothes." I was nine. I couldn't believe it. I said, "How can you expect me to do that? Washing clothes is your job. Anyway, all you have to do is to voice command it."

"Is that so?"

Mom walked around me then, walked around me like a bird to its prey. And then she said: "Okay, then you can voice command it. If you decide not to voice command it, then…" She waved her arm across the air, "…then you can wear what's already here."

"You mean the dirty ones?" I answered.

"You must like them to keep them where they are."

I had thought then that Mom had gone crazy, that all she cared about was a clean room, and not smelling the stink from my socks or something, but I was to quickly learn that was only the half of it. The other part had to do with teaching me a lesson – a lesson in cleaning.

That day, as one of the beasts dragged me to the 'chamber' this was all I could think about as I looked around me, waiting for my death. And then something else came to me. It was like a bright light entered my skull and I was seeing things clearly for the first time.

Mom had wanted me to learn responsibility.

Now, as I smelled the acrid smells of the chamber, and heard the aching drip of water knowing I would probably not be offered any, I thought of this, and I wondered what I could do with the knowledge now.

Perhaps it was everlastingly too late. Or maybe the memory came from fear; I would remember anything to cover up my forthcoming death. Maybe the smells of the room had triggered my thoughts. I wasn't sure. All I knew was I had to get out of this place.

Looking around me, I seemed to be alone. Where were Chandra, Neva, and Stella at a time like this? Perhaps we had been dragged into different rooms, awaiting our own torture.

The room was lit, but just barely, from what I couldn't tell, and the walls were made of glass like the others from Spectra. So, what was this place anyway? Besides a place of holding children against their will?

I tried to remove myself from the strap around my middle and crimped around my legs, tried to imagine that they dissolved at my very thought, but they remained fast. They seemed to be made of some sort of metal, a metal I couldn't break through. I thought of Neva. "Can you hear me?" I spoke inside my head. "Stella, are you there?" … "Chandra, where are you?" "…Mom…Dad?"

But the words didn't leave my brain. In fact, they seemed to echo within my head and bounce off one another. I closed my eyes, hoping for some relief, but the relief never came. I soiled myself once or twice and tried not to think about the humiliation. I cried, thinking of my mother and father.

I wondered if I had died.

But I wasn't dead. The beasts had come back into the chamber, and they were talking to each other in a language I didn't understand. The female Ursus hadn't returned, but the smell of the room was like rotting fruit amplified. I choked.

My right arm hung at my side. I still couldn't move it, and the right side of my body felt like it had been kicked – multiple times.

Finally, I heard a voice.

"It is time, human," it said.

Lifting my head, I looked into the beast's eyes, but all I saw were teeth. "So, you are the chosen one," It said. "I bet you feel pretty chosen now."

I spit. I was amazed that I still could.

The beast closed its mouth, wiping the edges with its hairy arm. "Come with me!" the bear-beast said, undoing my straps. I collapsed, but he held me.

Dragging me to the entryway of the chamber, the beast took me, alone, around the winding tunnel. I was just a bug, a fly, a mouse, and the thing was dragging me to who knows where. I hoped, no prayed, it wasn't a pit or that they would pull me apart from arm to arm. Poison would be best, like the poison that had been served up to Master Lorm. If I could choose a death, that would have been it.

With bleary eyes, I watched as the beast pulled me to a stop.

"How will I die?" I managed to ask.

The beast smiled. "You want to die then?"

"Isn't that why you've brought me to this place?" I looked around but saw nothing but glass walls. "Where is the death chamber?" I asked. "Make it quick."

"There. Look up."

Like Spectra, the place held an opening to the surface. I couldn't see it with my eyes, but my heart felt like it was there.

"Why have you brought me here? Why – "

A hairy hand was suddenly brought to my lips. I tried not to cough. It pressed against my lips, and all I could think about was how to bite it.

"There is not much time. With the little power you have left, and the power remaining in me, we can make it to the surface."

Kathryn Elizabeth Jones

The Guardian

At that moment I knew who held me, but how?

My eyes burned as I closed them, and as I thought about reaching the surface, we were there. "The plane!" the beast muttered. In a flash I was standing at the console with a weary Chandra collapsed at my feet.

I was more than shocked as we took off, leaving behind my parents and my best friends. Only when we could no longer see the red planet, did I place the plane in 'hover,' and look down at my feet.

Crouching, I stroked Chandra's hand. "Wake up!" I said.

She didn't stir.

I lifted her into my arms, feeling the pain of my broken arm all the way up to my neck. Lying her down on her bed, I placed my good hand on the right side of her face. Closing my eyes, I thought of her. I thought of all she meant to me. A warmth unlike I'd ever felt before ran through my fingers and to her skin.

She blinked. When her green eyes opened, the tears from my eyes had already reached my neck. I didn't wipe them. "You're alive!" I said.

She smiled and sat up. "What happened?"

"We're in the spaceplane. We've escaped," I said.

She touched my arm, the one that was supposed to be broken and no longer was. "Again?" she offered. "We seem to be doing that a lot."

I smiled back at her. "I know. Maybe I don't need the stone after all."

She got a funny look on her face then, funnier than I'd ever seen it. Placing her human hands on the bed she pushed herself off and stood on her feet. "Your parents?" she asked. "Oh, now I remember. We came without them."

"And Neva and Stella?" I asked.

"It's called Spore. I should have told you."

It was a creepy name. Actually, it sounded like a creepy mushroom or something, but I didn't say anything out loud to Chandra.

"It's a germ cell," Chandra replied. "That's all the Ursus think of when it comes to the children. Raising them up to the individuals they want them to be."

"A cell that will do their bidding," I replied.

"Much more than that. The children will be the new breed. They will be the 'second' breed."

"They will be Cyborg?" I asked.

"Yes. You probably noticed that the Ursus breed have no children of their own."

Actually, I hadn't noticed. "So, they want to create their own children from the monophyla?"

"It sickens me to think about it, but, yes. Their breed is quickly dying out. They tried to save themselves, of course, through transference, but even machine parts get worn out and stop working eventually."

"And that's why they want the stone?"

"How did you guess?"

Actually, I hadn't guessed. It just made sense. If the Ursus breed had powers of telekinesis. If they could walk through walls, and through their cyborg transference, extend their life, but not live forever, if they could even move objects without a thought, what was left but the power the stone had to never die?

Chandra placed her arm around me. "The best news is that the stone can't be used without faith, and faith is something the Ursus breed severely lack. You have just begun to use the powers of invisibility and transportation, and now can do these things on your own, but I'm afraid the ultimate power of the stone must be in hand for the ultimate gift to be realized."

"What gift? What gift does the stone have that allows the person to live forever?" It was finally time to know the truth; I could feel it under my skin. The warmth burned, and though not hot, it prickled against my flesh.

"Come with me."

I followed Chandra into the 'room' and we stood in front of the console. "Place your hands here, in this position," she said, directing my hands to the upper part of the screen.

"Where?" I asked because I couldn't see anything but metal. There was no button, no glowing place to press.

"Trust me. Push, here." She moved my hand to the top of the screen and pushed down with her palms. Instantly, the screen in front of me lit up. I jumped back. Chandra's face filled the screen, and she was speaking.

"I am the Guardian," she began. "I am forever. I am the universe." She smiled on screen, and it was the same smile I knew so well. Instinctively, I reached for Chandra's hand. She was still in human form standing next to me. "As the skies darken and are lit, as day follows night, as we reach for the light descending, we will heal our world. The green stone, and the power within it is our last hope."

She paused on the screen for a moment, as if looking over a vast congregation.

"There is one who has been chosen. One who will end all war. His name is Aaden."

I took a breath in, waiting for Chandra to continue. In seconds her voice was ending her message – a message of hope. "We once saw the past, the present and the future as one. We were one. And now, today, as I travel to Earth to retrieve the stone, my thoughts will be with you. I don't know what I will find, the difficulties

I will face, but I will find the stone, and I will find Aaden. Our Guardian."

The screen flipped to black and I turned to Chandra, still holding her hand. I wanted to kiss her at that moment, but all I could manage was a hug. She was warm, and all I could think about was how much I loved her.

Finally managing to pull away, I looked into her green eyes. "I love you, too," she said. "And now, now that you know the ultimate gift, we must go down and rescue those we love."

She was right. Only the first part of our plan had been put into place, and now would come the most difficult part of all.

Gathering the supplies for our journey was the easy part. Flying the space plane to our destination proved a bit more difficult. Not that I'd forgotten how to fly it, I was suddenly aware that we were no longer alone in space.

A huge ship, more than twice the size of our own, was suddenly before us.

Chandra gasped.

"Invisibility!"

The button pushed; we cruised the skies until the large ship was suddenly before us again.

"They see us!" I said.

Without warning, the space plane heaved and moved forward as if being pulled by a large magnet.

"They're taking us," she said. "We don't have the power…"

Shutting my eyes, I talked to the plane.

In the next second, we were pried from the hull.

"Now!" Chandra shouted. As the space plane raced the way we had come, all I could think about was the plan, but Chandra was quickly sensing my emotions.

"To the third planet!" she wailed. "To Sever!"

"Sever?" I shouted, taking note of the sky map before me.

"Land amongst the ruins."

I had no idea what Chandra was talking about, (Was this part of the plan? Was I forgetting something?) But then, as we neared the planet and the large ship no longer followed us, I saw it. "The Iron Pillar of Delhi."

The space plane *burred* to the ground. "Listen," Chandra said, touching my hand, "before we go out there, you need to know something."

"Like why the large ship didn't follow us?"

"More than that. Can you listen to me?"

I was suddenly transported back in time. "Yes, I can listen," I said, staring over at her. She'd suddenly changed into her monophyla form and was reaching up.

"There are many dead here," she said. "But one yet remains alive to help us. The Gupta King.

"Alright."

Chandra hopped on my shoulder as a monophylum. It was the first time she'd placed herself there and I wondered why, but there was no time to answer my question. We transported to the surface, and I was surprised to see a monophylum waiting for us. There were no guards, no Ursus breed, and no monophyla other than the one. In an instant, I knew him.

He reached forth his green hand and took mine. "Aaden, you have come at last," he said.

The Gupta King

The Gupta king smiled at me and I knew who he was. You never forget an old friend, even when you best remember him young, human, and much younger than the day he was shot out into space at his death. It's funny, but I was suddenly remembering Legos.

"I can't believe it's you," Bronty said.

"You're a monophylum!" I answered.

He placed his green hand on mine. "The monophyla saved me, changed my form."

"I want you to…"

"No problem." My friend suddenly turned into the boy I knew. I hugged him. "Bronty! So, it is you!" I cried, holding him tightly and whimpering like a baby. But I didn't care. It was Bronty!

"I like my human form, but I also like being monophylum. Those here, let's just say they prefer it, too."

I released myself from my friend. "How many are there?" I asked.

"Not many." He looked over at Chandra and reached out his human hand. "It's alright," he said. "We're the only ones on the surface at the moment."

In a blink, Chandra was in human form. "So, you do know each other. I thought you might."

Chandra had a wicked smile on her face. I knew then that she'd known all along that he was here, though I wondered why she hadn't told me.

"We have had much to do," she answered. "I couldn't have you visiting your friend instead of saving all monophyla."

She was probably right, and I was suddenly noticing the heat, though in my heart of hearts I knew I would have saved Dad first. But now he was gone from me once again.

Bronty directed us to the pillar. "I'm sorry the initial plan wasn't realized, but maybe we can help."

For an instant, I wondered how a bunch of old monophyla could do much of anything, and then I quickly changed my mind. The look of death from Bronty was reason enough.

We emerged into the tunnel and traveled down a long passageway to our destination.

"Fortunately, for all of our sakes, we have little to no intervention from the Ursus breed," Bronty said. "They come, but only rarely, supposing we aren't any kind of threat."

We emerged into a well-lit room (I was beginning to think that the light must come from the glass walls because there was no other fixture in the room) and to a wooden table surrounded by four chairs. "Goldilocks," I said before thinking.

"This is serious," Chandra offered, not missing a beat.

"Sorry," I said again, thinking over my multiple failures, one of them not taking things seriously enough when it was important.

"So, why didn't the others follow us?" I asked first.

"I think they may have," Bronty offered, looking again briefly at Chandra. "They have a cloaking device."

"Then, where are they? Why didn't they shoot us out of the sky?"

"Consider, Aaden. They can't get that stone to work without *you*."

I looked over at my friend. "This is so weird," I said. "I know you're Bronty, but you're acting so old. It does things with my brain."

"I know. And I'm sorry about that, but we need to use all of the time we have."

"Where are the others?" I asked.

Chandra blinked over at me, as if to say, not again… when Bronty spoke: "There are only a few of us now. Many have died. Only twenty-five of us at last count – ten males, fifteen females.

I was sorry I'd asked.

"The best news is that those who have remained are the healthiest among us. With their assistance…"

"We had plans to take the stone with the help of the children," I said. "Hopefully my parents and Slew and Stella are getting that done."

"The distance is far," Bronty said. "I have been trying to feel them for some time; I have tried to discover their progress with no success. Not having the stone has presented some problems for us."

"We can't do anything about that right now," Chandra said. "All we can do is hope that the others were successful."

Chandra was still in human form and I liked it. Bronty hadn't changed back either, and for all intents and purposes, we could have been talking around the dinner table on Earth. Still, I had no idea how we were going to work our way back to Spectra.

"I know your concerns," Chandra said, looking briefly at Bronty, "But we must find our way back. We know they will not kill you; no one else of their species has been able to work the stone that I know of, and they need you as their power source so to speak."

So, I was electricity now.

Bronty smiled at me. "You are indeed our light," he said. "Are you hungry?"

I nodded.

In that instant, a bowl of mush was brought to me from a female monophylum with a familiar spoon. I didn't care. I was just glad to have something. The two with me had been brought a cup of water, at least that's what I thought it was. Like their plant ancestors before them, all they needed was sun, water, and shelter when the occasion arose – like now. It seemed strange not to have my friend eat with me, but he was partly or mostly monophyla now, and I needed to remember that.

For a moment we didn't speak. Filled, Bronty stood, changed back to his monophyla form, and hopped on my shoulder. He was old, I knew that, but at least where the action was concerned, he seemed quite young. I was about to compliment him on his strength when he said:

"This is a secret, you hear? The Ursus know nothing of our physical prowess."

"What?" I asked. I had no idea what prowess was, but I figured the word had to do with brute strength of some kind.

"Never fear. There may only be a few of us who have yet to pass to the other world, but the few of us who are here will help you."

"How, with only one plane?"

Bronty smiled widely. "Only one plane? We have been building for years here."

I was surprised. "But where have you hidden them?"

"Interestingly, the Ursus have the opinion that the old, whether human or plant, can't do anything but sit and rock in their chairs. Fortunately, we discovered this early on, and when they've visited (very occasionally, mind you) we proved them right by sitting around."

"But they can walk through walls, read minds."

"So can we, and we've learned a thing or two about blocking our thoughts."

I was impressed as well as excited. With more planes, we could bring the suffering home. Although part of the plan had included bringing everyone to this planet, I just hadn't understood how we were going to do it without making multiple trips. Now, with multiple planes, the plan could actually be realized.

I turned to Chandra. "Did you know about this?" I asked.

"No, but I had a feeling something was going on here. Without the stone, things have been a bit hazy, especially where distance is concerned. But I knew that something was up."

"The messages were sent your way," Bronty continued, jumping off of my shoulder and taking his place once again at the head of the table. "We hoped you would hear them."

"And we have. Thank you."

Bronty bowed. "It has been the greatest pleasure to serve you, Guardian," he said. He turned to me. "You are my dearest friend."

"Will you ever really be young again?" I asked, for the thought of Bronty staying old with his old thoughts and young actions bothered me. I wanted the Monty I'd grown up knowing. Perhaps this was a selfish thought, but I couldn't help myself.

Bronty smiled. "I know. I feel the same way," he said. "But we must focus on what we can do. And right now, it's saving the monophyla on Spectra and Spore. We have been *sev*ered from society – thus our planet's name – but we will yet show the Ursus breed the truth of who we are."

The spaceplanes were fairly large; about the size of five passenger planes from my grandma's day and they were large enough to fit the many whom I knew would want to escape the clutches of Grude and his band. Still, there was the subject of the stone.

How would we get it without being seen? Even invisible, we could be watched. Our thoughts could be heard, and our desires made known.

"We have our ways," Bronty instructed, standing again and directing Chandra and me to the opening. "Follow me."

As in previous underground tunnels, we passed multiple lit and darkened chambers, and finally arrived at one filled with monophyla's. Those within were old to be sure, but there was something bright and shining in their eyes that told me that their outer appearance was only a façade – in reality, they had always been youthful beings of the monophyla race.

I thought about my own plants at home, the ones my mother had nourished and spoken with. I considered my first view of Neva as he spoke to me on Earth. I thought about our journey here, and about the monophyla, we'd found. They were growing still, moving forward and evolving into the beings they always were.

I couldn't help but be proud and grateful at the same time.

I stood before them, and they looked so small at my feet. But their green eyes blinked up at me, and their mouths smiled in that crooked way that I had first seen coming from Neva's thin lips. Everything would be alright; it just had to be.

The Dark Blue

I know I've shared with you some pretty unbelievable things, from spaceships to space beings and gifts that could only be conceived of as fantasy. But I want you to know that it is all real.

There was a time I didn't think this day would come to pass. As we centered ourselves on our upcoming journey – the 25 monophyla' s from Sever, myself, Chandra, and my long-time friends, Neva and Stella, we prayed for protection.

That same God you worship, we worship.

The stone would be gathered, but we, all of us, needed to clear our thoughts and replace them with the thoughts only the Ursus bread could hear. It was a lie, all of it, and I wondered again how Neva, with his secrets about his previous master's death, would fair now – now that we would be lying again.

We sat in a room with the others, learning how to empty our minds. It's what Stella had done before she'd become Stella when she'd lied about taking the thoughts from my mind when she hadn't. It was sort of middle-eastern, this practice. A sort of meditation, like those done on Earth before its destruction.

"Empty your minds," Bronty began. "Remember your growth, your childhood, when everything was new. Clear your mind of judgment; you have none. Clear it of fear, of purpose other than the basic necessities of eating, drinking and sleeping. You are a child now. You are one with your maker."

My own mind swirled with so many things in the beginning. How my father and mother were doing on Spore. If they'd managed to find the children. If the word had been spoken that we'd be coming for them. I thought about my childhood, but my mind was mixed-up with other things. The destruction of the Earth, the space plane; even the astronauts in silver who had not wanted us to travel at first.

When Bronty placed his green hand on my leg as I sat still on the floor of the room, I jumped, opened my eyes, and looked over at him.

He shook his head and continued around the room.

"All of us, even those with advanced powers, must rely on the emptiness of their birth, and their first knowledge. Remember when even a blade of grass caused you to discover it? When the sun was warm on your arms and you wondered why…"

In time, I felt like I was ready. Thoughts of emptiness were replaced with thoughts only the Ursus breed would think. Thoughts of power. Thoughts of war. Thoughts of death.

I cried myself to sleep most nights following a cleansing, and the morning we stepped aboard the space planes – me, Chandra, Neva, and Stella, to the one we knew by heart, and the others, to those they had built on the planet, Sever – I felt ready.

But you know how it feels to be ready, when, in reality, your readiness is not real. If you understand how it feels to be prepared to give a speech at school and then tremble as you stand before your class. If you know how it feels to walk into a new school with all eyes on you, or the pain and ultimate healing of a fall, you may know how I felt that day the space plane took off and I wondered if we'd triumph.

We reached the red planet, Spectra, before the heat had manifested itself to its highest burn. The spaceplanes were hidden behind the tall brush, our thoughts – Ursus. We were invisible, and yet the time would come when we'd show ourselves as Ursus in the flesh.

Yes, we would also become Ursus, like Chandra had become when we'd escaped from the planet, Spore.

We would not only be thinking Ursus, but we would also be presenting ourselves *as* Ursus.

"Reveal yourselves," Bronty said as we landed. "Your thoughts and appearance will have to be perfect. I'm sorry this has come so soon."

A chill of fire raced up my back. So, we wouldn't have time to practice our delusion; the time was now.

Stepping from the craft with Neva and Stella beside me, I prayed for Chandra. She was the first. There were at least eight of the Ursus breed that I could see. As my skin adjusted to the heat from the planet's surface, and my eyes took in the creatures before us, I thought of those things that I had been taught.

"Your thoughts are dark as you land," said the largest among them. He walked haltingly closer to Chandra and reached out his hairy paw.

She took it. "And you, you were not expecting us. I can explain."

The Ursus grunted. "I am Curl. Have you come to see the prisoners?" he asked.

"Yes," Chandra answered firmly. "Take us to them."

My thoughts continued. I thought of torture, pain, death and anything else that an Ursus would be thinking at a time like this.

"You will have to wait, I'm afraid," said Curl, walking ahead of us, but behind his comrades who he'd signaled to go ahead. "The humans, they are difficult.

Some of the monophyla children have gone missing. We hear their voices but have not, as yet, located them."

When Chandra hesitated, Curl continued: "You have not come from the Great One?"

"We have come to deliver a message."

I thought of Grude then, but not in the way you might be thinking. Instead of my normal thoughts of him, all I could manage was a fairly weak thought about my great reverence for him."

Curl stopped at that moment and turned to me. "You do not see Grude's value, then?" he asked, staring me down. "His mate – the immortal Presda may be pleased. She no longer caters to him either."

I took in a deep breath.

We followed the nine to the Iron Pillar, the door opened, and in moments we were inside.

"She will ask you about your mission," Curl began as we traversed the tunnels. "She will ask you why it has taken you so long to return from Earth. I hear it is no more."

I gulped, trying not to release the images of my time there. Instead, I filled my mind with hateful thoughts of humans and how they deserved to die.

"You are right," said Curl, and I knew my cover-up had been successful. "The two here are more trouble than they're worth. They escaped once, but when found all we could retrieve from their minds was that the children were in hiding."

"We will know where they are soon enough," Chandra said, placing her furry paw on Curl's shoulder. "To the death of all humans!"

"To the death!" he repeated.

A sudden light filled my Ursus eyes. We stepped inside. The chamber was like nothing I had previously seen. Instead of glass walls, the surface appeared to be gold. The table was not wood, but sort of silver metallic. The chairs matched. On the walls hung colored tapestries, golden medals of decapitated heads, and a sampling of what looked like food hanging over our heads.

"So, you have come to visit me from Earth?" Presda asked," reaching for a silver strand of something with a piece of what looked like meat hanging from the end. She sucked it inside her mouth. "Did you bring any Earth creatures?" she asked.

"We did not, glorious one. They are all dead."

"No fresh blood?"

"No. The Earth is gone."

I took in another deep breath. Tears glistened in my eyes for only an instant, but that instant had been long enough for Presda to notice.

"And you? Who are you?" she asked.

"I am Null," I said as we'd rehearsed.

"Null and void," Presda laughed.

I stood firm. It wasn't proper to laugh back.

"What sort of parents would give you such a terrible name?"

"My parents have met up with the afterlife."

"And they were?"

"Hebta and Bail."

"And you?" She looked straight on to Chandra.

"I am Countess."

"Now, here's something." Presda arose and walked mechanically to her. "And your parents?"

"Shorn and Nesta."

"Better. You must be the pilot."

"Yes," Chandra lied.

"You're fairly small."

"My strength comes from within," Chandra said truthfully.

"I can see that," Presda answered, stepping closer.

"How come you are late?"

"Ship problems from the surface of the planet," Chandra spoke truthfully again. "We barely escaped with our lives."

"Sit."

We sat and in moments were given permission to eat. I had no idea what I was eating, something stringy, but I ate. I filled my mind as full as I could with Ursus thoughts and focused on thinking the meal delicious.

Cups of liquid were brought to us. With my first sip, I knew it wasn't punch.

"The sap and skin of the monophyla's leave much to be desired, but the time will come when we'll have something better. I am hoping with pleasure for that day."

I couldn't think it, I just couldn't. I'd heard Earth stories of eating your own kind. As the thought burst forth into my brain, I thought of something else – anything else – the mate of Presda.

"So – you know him, do you?" Presda asked. "Most of our breed does. So, what do you think of him? Is he the grand ruler you expected? Or were your expectations dissolving the moment you met him?"

"I... I... he is a great leader of the Ursus breed," I said.

"Why do you hesitate? Tell me what you really think of him."

Now things were getting a bit easier. "He is a weak tyrant. A power monger. A..."

Presda stood in anger, shaking the silver table. "What do you mean, he's a power monger? I am that, only me!"

"What I meant to say..."

"You must have been away for a long time, not to see my superiority in this and every way!"

"My apologies..."

"You think to apologize? Why? Isn't your word as gold?"

"Yes." I tried to make my voice firm.

"Good. Then you will hold to it. Now, allow me to give you a tour of the prisoners. I would give you one for keeping, but I've been instructed... to hold off for a time. Grude... he is an impatient one, so we will be still, at least for now."

As we stood, all I could do was think of war and death and hate. As we followed Presda out of the glittering chamber, I continued to think about these things until my stomach burned from the pain of it. But I remained silent. We all remained silent.

"Hail, Presda!"

The voices were strong as we entered the holding chamber to behold our friends. My father and mother were pinned to the wall with some sort of silver holding device, Neva and Stella were pinned to the floor. I made my mind numb as well as my heart. I looked at them as if they were merely something to eat.

"You see, they are still here, as instructed."

Presda licked her lips.

"Are they being fed?" I asked.

"You ask such a question? Search their minds for yourself."

I did as I was told but could find nothing that would help us in what needed to happen next. I didn't dare relay a message to my parents about anything, and, anyway, they were in some sort of dream state, their eyes closed.

"Now, to your sleeping chamber!" Presda grunted, leading us out. I didn't dare look back or think anything. Part of me was happy that they hadn't opened their eyes upon our arrival. I knew Neva and Stella could hide their true feelings, and maybe even my parents, but I doubted if I could.

Leaving the opening we traveled the tunnel until we'd made our way to our chamber.

"Grude is asking for a report."

Presda turned and left us. I turned to Chandra.

"Wait," she mouthed.

I stood in silence waiting. Finally, Chandra said: "She is far from us now, and will only be able to hear us if she tunes in. She is busy speaking with Grude. We don't have much time."

"Grude will know that we come under false pretenses," I said, thinking of my cleverness in using big words.

"You must be silent. Continue your thoughts of hate as I speak with you."

"He will not know at first. Many space planes were sent to Earth, but not many have returned. If anything, he will be feeling surprised that we have returned. He will be eager to ask us questions."

I nodded.

"Your parents look tired, so do Neva and Stella. I'm not sure if they'll have the energy to release the children."

"Where are the children?"

"I don't know, at least not yet. How are you feeling?"

"Surviving."

"Do you feel strong enough to heal your parents?"

I nodded.

"You must be sure. I can help some, but you must believe that all things are possible."

"All things."

I reached for father. Placing my hands on his I thought of the healing words. They were unspoken but I knew they could still be heard. After a few moments, my father opened his eyes in recognition. I touched his lips, silencing him, and turned to my mother, placing my hands on hers. She did not revive, and so I tried again.

"Allow me to help you," Chandra said, placing her furry fake fingers over my own. She closed her eyes. There was a greater pain in my mother than in my father and I wondered why, but in seconds it came to me. Mother was female.

Her weakness was also her strength.

We quickly turned to Neva and Stella, but by then, my own weakness was plainly evident; Chandra finished for me. As my friends' eyes blinked open, I felt something caress my skin. It breathed out its hate even before I heard the words.

"I thought so," Presda said, taking me by the arm, and pulling me aside. "You have brought the others; I can feel them."

I thought of the hate I felt for Presda in just that moment, no amount of pretending was necessary. Still, she held me tight. Yelling at the guards, Chandra was soon taken, but not before I saw my friend Bronty on the other side of the wall. He, along with others of the pretended 'first breed' was ready to pounce.

"You think the old will help you? I have felt your ships even before you landed. I knew about your plan, and I am here to stop you."

My father blinked up at me and I realized at that moment, that my cover-up had truly been revealed. I was no longer an Ursus.

Informer

"Aaden!" Mother gasped, as the beast dragged me from the room.

Out the opening, I blinked over at Bronty and the others standing near them.

Bronty smiled and reached for me. Presda's eyes glittered.

"If not for your friend… this day may not have occurred," Presda spit.

I looked into Bronty's eyes as he revealed himself.

"I'm sorry," he began.

For a moment I didn't understand anything. It was like I was frozen, as still and un-life-like as the pillar that graced every land inhabited by these beings. And then I knew the truth. My skin prickled at the thought, and my heart did something it had never done before. "Sorry, sorry?" I yelled, my eyes burning into the one green eye of my trusted friend.

Presda's mouth curled up, and her arms, fur and all raised to her sides. "Because of your help to the Ursus breed your foodstuffs will be increased; your way of life preserved."

I continued to look into Bronty's eyes. "We are old," he said, "and will soon die out. We will be no more."

"I thought you were my friend!"

"I can no longer be your friend. I must…"

Now my heart was truly filled with hate. "You led me here, you coerced me to this place. And all, for what? To see me dead?"

Bronty blinked, and a small tear fell from his eye. Behind him, the other monophyla stood and all I could think about was how much I hated them all.

"Good, this is very good," Presda said, pulling me back to her side. All I could smell was fruit, decaying fruit. She would put me in my cell, but before I died, I would make myself throw up. I would get rid of it all, every last bit of it, and I would hate them all to my last breath.

Pushing me back into the room, I fell at the feet of my father. Neva was to me in an instant, caressing my hand.

"Clamp them! Tomorrow's feast will be a glorious one!" Presda shouted. She laughed deeply, like a cave that continued on forever with no way out.

Mom wasn't well. Though I had healed her with Chandra's help, her skin was pale. She was thin and I could almost see the bones protruding from her arms and legs. Father looked better, but not by much. His silver suit had been replaced by something else – something foreign and brown. It covered his body like a great cocoon.

Neva and Stella fared better, but their skin had turned a yellow-green and I knew it wouldn't be long before tree sap would be desperately needed. Neva caressed my face. Stella was at my feet.

"You have used up your strength," she said. "What will we do now?"

"I don't know." I didn't want to cry, I didn't want to appear weak, but what did it matter now? We would soon die, all of us, and nothing else would matter anymore. I hadn't saved the planets here; I hadn't saved the breed of creatures I had grown to love.

"You must listen," Neva said.

"No more listening! When I see Presda next, I will kill her!"

"Your mind is full of hate."

Mother touched my hand but I didn't feel anything but hate. So, they had done it after all. Filled me with what I only thought would be temporary. My friend, my longtime friend, had informed on me. He had told the others of our coming. He had lied to me.

I couldn't cry. I couldn't do anything but sit there and hate them all.

When the Ursus finally released us, I had no idea how much time had passed, but I didn't care. I didn't think of my powers charging up – hadn't the green stone taken a day or two to regain its power? I could feel Mother's breath on my back, and the way my father slid his feet as if walking was difficult. Neva was no longer on my shoulder, but I could feel them both near me, their limbs changing from yellow to white. Death would come to all of us.

The tunnel was damp. I could smell water dripping, though I couldn't see it. We passed one room that looked as if it was a place for eating, and I instantly remembered the hanging plants that had fed us from the ceiling the first time. Another opening revealed monophyla in service, yet another, a place for sleeping. But none of it mattered. Now.

Near the near end of the tunnel, we turned and were deposited into a great room, larger than I'd seen before. We were clasped to pieces of metal coming from the glass walls.

A large beast entered: Grude. "So, you thought to fool me, is that it?" he began, licking his lips. I couldn't see Presda anywhere, but there were plenty of Ursus feeding against the walls. Curl, Presda's main guard, was standing by the entrance. I was beginning to see the differences in the species even though I still hated them. Where Grude's face was full and Presda's slimmer, Curl had a larger nose. He winked at me now, smirking in believed superiority.

"Come to attention!" Grude growled. "This will be a great feast, but we must prepare ourselves." He held out the green stone.

It had been days since I'd last seen it, and now I truly couldn't take my eyes off it. Had it dimmed with time? The stone was no longer green. More than two days had obviously passed, and it was still black.

I breathed slowly, taking in everything before me; the Ursus, my family, the walls, even the scraps of monophyla parts decaying on the floor throughout the room. I felt stronger than the day before, but not by much, and I knew I wouldn't be able to release any of us now.

The beast held up the stone. "Today is the day of beginnings. Of life!" He looked at me, his red eyes swimming with hate.

I knew all about hate – now. I knew all about death. My parents were silent. They had spoken little the night before, and I didn't even care. Just like I didn't care now.

"Aaden's life may be saved, if for one thing."

I knew what that one thing was but I was too filled with hate to tell him anything. Their breed would never know.

"But we already know the secret," Grude said, stepping closer. "You think to hide it but hiding anything now will prove fruitless."

I almost laughed at the beast. Sniffing the air, I said, "Do you ever bathe?"

This appeared to take the beast by surprise. He blinked at me, once, then stared into my eyes as if he could pierce them with just a look, and then his voice calmed. "So, you know we can read minds. Walls are no encumbrance. We can move things with just a thought…"

"You will die like everyone else," I said, clenching my teeth. "You are part machine, but you will break down. You will die."

I couldn't have said anything worse. The beast rose on his toes, and still holding the stone, tossed it at me. I missed the catch and the stone hit my face, just below my right eye, causing blood to drip to my feet.

Walking haltingly to the stone, and me, Grude picked it up, but not before spitting into my face.

"So, you think you're beyond the stone," he said.

I remained silent, the heat within me burning like an iron skillet.

"I am," I lied. For at that moment, that time of death, I thought it was a lie. I thought it was all over. Let the beast eat me. Let him take me from my family and friends. I knew I would be dead, and that my spirit form could never be touched. I believed in God. God would save me.

"Who is God?" Grude shouted.

I blinked. "God?" I asked.

"I have never heard of him," Grude said, breathing down on me, the stone in his paw. "Can he help you with this stone?"

It was the first time in days I'd thought to consider it. *Yes,* I spoke in my mind. *You have to be humble to use it. Pride cannot enter your heart. You have to have faith.*

"What is faith?" the beast asked.

I turned to my mother. She was right next to me on the glass wall, followed by my father, Stella, and Neva at the end.

"Tell him," she said.

I blinked. This moment was a far cry from Sunday School but maybe it would work.

"Faith is to believe in things you can't see," I started.

"Like invisible things," the beast answered.

"Sort of."

"What do you mean?" he heaved. "Is it like walking through walls, transporting yourself above ground?"

"Sometimes."

The beast yelled. The walls rumbled. I thought they might break.

"I have felt hate in you. I have felt death. I have also felt the weakness you humans and monophyla call love."

145

I was surprised at the beast's words. I wasn't sure what to say.

"You will not be able to use it," I finally offered. "It takes… faith. Something you don't have."

"And something you have lost," the beast answered.

My blackened heart jumped inside my chest.

"If what you say is true, this stone is useless to me."

I nodded.

"Then, you will die!"

The beast's teeth gnashed, and it was all I could do to keep my voice steady. So, this was my choice then, to live with a blackened heart, or to let all of the hate go."

"You can let it go, then. I knew it. How?"

I felt Neva at that moment, whispering in my ear. It was a feeling more than words. I felt it from Stella, too, and from my mother and father. If I had to die, now, at least I would die with everyone I truly cared about.

"Hand me the stone, and I'll show you," I said.

"You'll teach me of the past, present, and future?" Grude asked.

"I will."

The beast hesitated for a moment as I filled my soul with the love I needed for this task. I knew I couldn't love this wicked beast, but I could focus on those I did love, and in this, we could all be saved.

In a blink, the beast was smiling. "You think to trick me," he said. He turned, and, walking to the entrance, brought forth a monophyla plant. The thing was alive and a sickly purple. He didn't speak, but in an instant, I knew who he was – the death camas – the poisonous one. The one whose ancestors had killed Master Lorm, Neva's master.

"So, you are feeling better, are you?" Grude asked.

"I don't know what you mean," I lied, though I had felt it myself, the moment my blackened heart had jumped within my chest and I knew there was still hope for me.

"You will live without them," the death plant uttered. His voice was shrill, like an old saw needing oiling. It was the strangest, frightening thing I'd ever heard.

If you're thinking right now that I had no choice, that I had to show the beast the ultimate power, you'd be completely right. But there is something about truth that a beast like Grude and a plant like the death camas would never understand.

A Shot in the Dark

"Now!" Bronty shouted.

His voice was more than music, it was power, and the power shattered the glass walls and opened the clamps.

Rushing to Grude, I reached the blackened stone. It turned green at my touch. In the moments that hate had filled the heart and mind of Grude and I'd spoken about the power of love, I'd felt something else. I hadn't made room for it, knowing that the beast would see it, but the thing had filtered through the air above me like a hot air balloon.

Bronty had tricked us all, and I was glad.

Pushing the stone into my pocket, I reached for my parents, for my friends. As the beasts moved toward us, we vanished, moving through the walls and transporting ourselves to the surface of the red planet, Spore.

The monophyla children, who had been collected by Bronty, rushed toward us. I'd never been hugged by so many plants in my life! And then we were rushing to the planes and finding a space in them for all of the children.

We weren't alone for long.

In seconds, the cyborg beasts, and the others in mid-transformation had discovered Bronty's deception and were running towards us, their huge hairy feet pounding the red sands. Their yells, like beasts on the warpath.

There wasn't time to think, just to move. As the last monophyla rushed inside the space plane and the hatch closed, I breathed a sigh of relief. But my sigh was short-lived. A hairy arm shoved its way into the opening and pulled open the door.

I hadn't really known the strength of the Ursus, but now we were all getting the biggest taste of it in our lives. As the door flew open, tossed angrily outside the space plane, the Ursus tumbled inside, each in turn, reaching for the nearest monophylum.

"Stop!" I screamed, but it was too late.

"We will all die!" Chandra huddled beside me, as one-two-three of her breed were thrown without the opening. Now all of the beasts were inside, including Grude who looked at me, hate burning in his red eyes.

"The stone!" he shouted, standing firmly in front of me.

He was tired, I could see that – his breathing shallow, but his legs were sturdy. His right paw was opened in front of him. "Tell me the truth, now!"

I felt the green stone within my fingers, played with it for only a second – a second too long.

"Now!" the beast shrieked again, or Chandra will die!"

He had her by her golden hair, for she was human again, and for all intents and purposes, as human as I'd ever seen her. Her green eyes filled with tears and blinked over at me. "Don't do it," she said.

"I will kill her!" Grude shrieked again, pulling my friend to the air and opening its mouth.

"Let him! Let him!" Chandra yelled.

The stone burned my fingers but I held it tightly within my fist. Closing my eyes, I made myself disappear, and with everything I had, jumped into the air. Taking the stone from my pocket, I pushed the glittering green stone into Grude's left eye.

He roared, dropping Chandra to the ground.

Grude reached for his eye, pulled the stone out of its socket, and released it to the ground. I grabbed the stone from the space plane floor and pulled Chandra to me. "To our freedom!" I yelled, holding the green stone high above my head.

If you want to know the truth, what happened next was not even close to being my own idea. In the next blink, the other monophyla had jumped on the shoulders of the Ursus, and they were pushing their slim green fingers into their red eyes.

I'm not sure when it had occurred to me that the red eyes held the power the Ursus used to control others; not even their brute strength could do what their eyes could – but at that moment I felt as if the monophyla understood too.

Presda hovered above me like a dark star, but in the next moment, the green stone was pushed into her eye. She collapsed at my feet, moaning incoherently.

I turned to see the next Ursus hurling itself at me. It appeared to be the guard who had kept us captive. His decayed breath filled my nostrils as the stone was pushed forward. But I had missed his eye. His arm reached around me and pulled me to him in a tight thrust. I could barely breathe.

"Let me go," I whispered in his ear, "and you shall have the power of the green stone."

The beast looked on me. I could see the scrape to the left of his eye where the stone had reached. He drew me closer. "Command the others to stop," he growled.

All were in an uproar. I looked down at the stone, dimming quickly before my very eyes. "Stop!" I screamed, but no one appeared to hear me.

The beast held me tighter.

"Stop!" I wailed again.

This time, Chandra held her hand up. "Stop!" she echoed, as beasts around me fell at my feet.

Below me, dozens of cyborg Ursus appeared to be dead, one eye or both, punctured at their sockets. It was a gruesome image, but I tried not to reflect on the blood, only on how I could kill the guard.

"You think to deceive me?" the beast asked, dropping me to the ground.

I stood and felt for the stone in my pocket. It no longer burned my fingers, and, as I pulled it from my pocket, I could see that the bright green glow had diminished. In its place was something resembling darkness.

I could no longer feel Bronty. I had felt him guiding me for quite some time, though he was far from my sight, and now that the stone had dimmed to blackness, I was truly alone. Chandra had been beaten. Though not killed as far as I could tell, she lay still beside me.

I had no idea where my parents were, and I supposed Neva and Stella – dead.

The fight had been great, but we appeared to be back where we started – in captivity. I was tired and angry, and no longer held the green stone, now black. So, it would need some time to recharge, and, in the meantime, I needed to heal in order to escape this place.

I tried to rouse Chandra with my thoughts, but she didn't move. Perhaps she was dead, and in a few moments, I would be killed as well. Perhaps the beasts were tired of waiting and would no longer wait for me to cooperate with them. But that couldn't be so, could it? Though at that moment I truly wanted to die. I was the only one who could help the Ursus breed with the power they felt they deserved, though I really had no idea how to use the past, present and future for even my own benefit.

I wondered why Chandra, the Guardian, hadn't told me, but perhaps, even she did not know, and the workings of the stone were up to me. If that was true, we were all in for a quick death.

Laughter reached my ears. A lone monophylum suddenly stood before me. It was gray-black like a decaying plant on Earth. The monophyla I had known had begun their deaths differently, the colors of a different shade altogether.

The plant opened its mouth to speak, the tunnels of its throat like something underground. "So, you think to tempt me with your seeming lack of knowledge?"

"Who are you?" I asked. I knew who stood there, its one green eye blinking.

"I am Camas," came the reply. It held out the stone. "Tell me about it."

The death camas didn't smile, didn't do anything but glare at me as it held out the stone. I knew the death camas was poison, and that it could kill anyone within its breath. But I knew I was safe, at least until I revealed the information. After that…"

"You worry for your life," the plant breathed. "I have a bargain to make."

I tried to sit up straighter, but my back hurt even as I lifted myself higher against the wall.

"Chandra, your dear Chandra is still alive, but she will die unless I learn the truth."

"But if I tell you the truth, you will kill me," I said. "I am not ready to die."

It was sort of a stupid remark. I looked ten after all, even though I was fifteen, and the plant before me only glowered as its green eye blinked.

"I will release you after I know the truth about the stone."

"Then Grude didn't tell you. You must be pure in heart to use it."

"Bah! That's why I have you," said Camas. "You will be my true light. You will show me the way. Anything can be tricked."

Saliva gathered on Camas' bottom lip. The thing licked it.

"Grude was weak; I am stronger."

"You defy your own kind?"

"I am my own kind!"

The walls thundered, and I hoped the glass behind me would not break.

"You have killed many then?" I queried.

"Many, including humans." Camas smiled then and rolled the stone in my direction. It stopped at my feet. Picking it up, I examined it. The stone remained black.

"Grude knew one thing. The stone took just a few hours to receive its strength. Perhaps you can coax it along."

"No," I said truthfully. "The stone needs at least a day."

"You are weak," it said.

"I am human," I answered.

The plant smiled again and walked closer to me. "Chandra was once powerful, but she couldn't surpass me. Even Grude, as powerful as he was, had to die, along with his mate."

"Presda is dead then?"

"At your hand. Tell me how you did it with the stone."

"No."

"I can read your thoughts. So, it was their eyes that held the power. I thought so."

"You didn't know?"

Camas stood rigidly before me. "How dare you contradict my power!"

I bowed my head in mock reverence. "I'm sorry," I said.

The plant was silent.

"You are strong for a human," Camas finally said.

Unlike humans, where the subject of gender was easily distinguished, the same wasn't true for the monophyla race. One knew the gender of the plant by observance mostly. The way the plant walked and spoke. Neva, for example, was more to the point, more direct; while Stella was more thoughtful, caring. In this way, the plants resembled similar human traits. Camas was definitely a 'he'.

"Tell me the truth of the stone, how to wield the power, and you will be released."

"And my parents?"

The plant hesitated. "And your parents."

"Neva and Stella? Chandra? The children?"

"You ask a lot."

"Not for what you are wanting," I replied easily, though the thought of the power that the death camas would wield scared me more than I could even think about.

"True. To be the master of all things past, present and future, will give me much more than what I offer you. Accepted."

"We must wait until the stone glows green," I said. "I will need sustenance. Chandra will need sustenance, as well as those you have held elsewhere."

The death camas smiled.

"So be it."

I could not read time, stuck as I was underground. But I did receive food, some sort of green plant and a drink like some sort of nectar. The taste of each was peculiar, almost sour, but I ate and drank to regain my strength.

It was near the time of eating again – a rough plate of food came twice a day just after I had relieved my bowels – and I figured we were in the second day when I noticed a slight glow from the stone.

"Chandra…" I whispered. "Are you awake?"

Surprisingly, Chandra sat. She placed her slim, green finger over her lips.

I thought about death, about darkness, about doing the will of Camas, but only to keep my mind from thinking of the plan that must have been forming in my brain without me even knowing it.

In an instant, I felt something else – something warm in which I tried not to focus on. And I knew he was there. I decided to keep quiet as the plate came in.

The being smiled and touched my hand.

Standing, I reached for Chandra. She stumbled in front of me, still held captive by her wrists, though in an instant the clasp was released.

She touched my shoulder and we wandered out.

Near the opening, Chandra placed her thin finger once again over her lips, and I thought of the journey ahead – but not too much. We followed Bronty out the opening, down the tunnel, and to the end of the corridor, stopping near the entrance.

Bronty went in. I hesitated with Chandra.

Perhaps the move was wise, for in only seconds Bronty had retrieved my parents and my two dear friends. They followed him out, but not before my mom's eyes found mine. "Don't even think it," I offered, and her eyes left mine.

We followed Bronty once more, down the tunnel, and to the place, I'd recognized as the way out. Touching the stone with my fingers, it burned. I closed my eyes, watching the others do the same. The journey seemed to take a long time. I was thankful to Bronty but wondered how long this cover-up would last. Camas was stronger than my other captors. He seemed to understand things on a far deeper and wicked level than his counterparts.

I breathed in the stagnant air of the tunnels, listening to the water drip from the unknown place, and I was almost convinced that we had done it, escaped the confines of this awful place when suddenly a green hand reached out.

"So, you think to escape your fate!" the voice hissed, pulling me to him. I couldn't breathe. In my pocket, I felt for the stone. "You will die, all of you!"

My mom screamed and fell at the feet of my father. Neva and Stella jumped on my shoulders and reached for the death camas. Like lint, they were plucked off and thrown to the ground.

I didn't know what to do. Could the stone lead the way?

Even in the thought, my answer came. Reaching for it, I turned, pushing the stone into the eye of our captor. "AAgh!" he screamed, releasing his grip on me.

159

The green stone was still in his eye and he was trying to dislodge it. "AAgh!" he howled again as the green stone burned his flesh. "Take it from me! Take it!"

The death camas fell then, bound into one of the glass walls. The wall rumbled but did not shatter. I reached for the stone. Plucking it from its eye, I placed the green stone in my pocket.

"Run!"

Other monophyla were yelling within the corridor.

"To the surface!" I screamed, closing my eyes, and feeling the separation of underground tunnels. A spark of heat stung my flesh as we arrived on the planet's surface.

"The planes are just around the bend!"

We ran.

I don't know how long we ran, but I could feel the heat of the stone leaving my palm and knew we'd used up most of its power getting everyone to the surface.

I didn't look behind me as I ran, and neither did the others, but I knew one thing. The monophyla who had been forced to serve the death camas were right behind us.

On the space plane, I rushed inside to see many others waiting. A cheer rang out before the door slid shut. I could feel the plane move, and in seconds we were above land, racing through the stars.

"Son! Son!" My mom had a way of worrying me faster than anyone else. "You're hurt!"

I looked down to see a pool of blood seeping through my stomach.

I wasn't sure what had caused it until Chandra said, "You have received the poison."

I was sitting near the control panel and looked at Chandra who had transformed herself into the girl with yellow hair. Behind her, sat my two friends, and they were bleeding as well.

"They have been touched by the death camas, and they will die," Chandra said.

"No!"

I stumbled to them, reaching for the stone in my pocket. It was black.

Neva was already yellow, his stem turning white as I looked on him. Stella wasn't faring much better. "I'm sorry," she said, reaching for me. She stopped her hand from touching my own. "You must live."

I touched my middle, unsure of what she could mean. I would die and they would die. I would be alright because in the afterlife we would be together.

"No. You are the Chosen One. You must not die," Neva said. He breathed heavily once, and I could see the air from his nostrils filling the space above him.

Again, I looked at the stone.

"Past, present, and future, what does it mean?" I asked.

"You already know," Neva said. "It's about love."

"What?" I blinked, tears filling my eyes and spilling to the ground. "Tell me!"

"You will find it. You are the only one who will be able to find it."

"Help them!" I shrieked to no one in particular, though many hovered around us now. We were in the air, seeking refuge from Camas, and my friends were going to die!"

I reached for them, touching their skin. "I will not let you die!" I shouted.

Chandra knelt beside me. "Tell me what to do," she said.

It was crazy, really, how she asked as if she was no longer the more powerful one with all of the answers. "But you-you are the Guardian!"

Chandra sniffed. I knew she was crying, but I had no idea what to tell her. I had no idea what to tell myself. The past, present, and future were all mixed up inside my brain, and I had no clue what it all meant. And then something came to me. It was the pillar – the same pillar that had been placed on each of the planets I'd visited. Were they something beyond a portal to the surface?

The iron pillar never got old – it never rusted – it had been used for the spacecraft I was flying in at precisely this very moment! It was heavy but lightweight and carried the name of Chandra in the third verse of the Gupta chant.

"How did the iron pillar come to be?" I asked.

"It has always been there, wherever we have gone," Chandra said.

I looked down at Stella. She was white. Her companion had lost all color. Death was imminent.

"Your name is also on the pillar," Chandra continued. "It is a testimony of the truth that you are."

"How can that be?" I sobbed, clasping my friends in my arms.

"You are the Chosen One."

"Chosen to do what?"

"To save us all!"

I prayed then, prayed harder and with more fervency than I'd ever prayed before. I prayed for my friends to live. I prayed that we'd escape the hands of the evil Camas. I prayed that I would know what to do. When I opened my eyes, I looked at the still forms of my two friends.

Mom was next to me, pushing something warm against my stomach. Her hand.

"We need to heal you of this wound!" she said.

"I can't!" I sobbed, throwing myself against Neva and Stella.

"You must!" Dad shouted, pulling me away.

With death, I am told, there is always something to learn, but I had no interest in learning it. My friends were dead, and I was close to it. I'd already stained my mother with the poison, and my father, carrying me to my bed, had stained the outside of his brown clothes; clothing that looked more like a sack to store very large potatoes in.

I watched as he ripped the thing from his body, throwing it into the corner. He was practically naked standing before me but I didn't care. Mom was crying, pouring what looked like water over her poisoned hand, but I knew that the water would not work. I would die, and then my mom would follow. Maybe Dad would survive.

Chandra was not with me. I was told she was in the 'room' fighting for our lives. The space plane rocked like a great giant in the air, and I knew that the death camas had followed us out here. If he couldn't get to the stone, he would kill us all. There was no question that the Ursus breed were helping him. Maybe they had been promised their own freedom.

Bronty might have been with Chandra, but I wasn't sure. There were many planes to fly now and I wasn't at all sure where anyone was being used.

We had saved the monophyla race, and I wondered how long it would take before we died. It wasn't that I didn't have confidence in our abilities, it's just that the opposition to life was so fierce I wondered how strong our force really was. I was thankful to Bronty for his strength and for Chandra's lead in getting me to this moment. Along with Neva and Stella, my parents had also given me the love I needed to keep going.

But now?

Death Camas

I must have been delirious because all I could think about was that my friends were alive and that, after all, I'd had a terrible, horrifying dream that wasn't real at all.

Opening my eyes, the first face I saw was my mother's. "So, you are stronger than you think," she said, brushing some stray hairs from my eyes, with a hand that didn't even hold a scar, nor any signs that I could see that she'd been poisoned. "It's about time for a haircut."

It was beyond time for a haircut, if the truth be known. Since leaving Earth I hadn't taken a snip at it once. It was as long as a girl's, and I'd had to pin it back with discarded pieces of rope. I hadn't had much time to look in a mirror either, but the times I had, I'd almost been brought to laughter.

I was a fifteen-year-old boy who looked like a ten-year-old girl.

"Neva? How is Neva?" I asked, trying to sit up. But the task of sitting was difficult, if not bordering on insanity.

"Lay down. You still need time."

"How many days have I been out?"

"Three."

"Three!"

My eyes blinked at the thought of it. I had been asleep for three days?

"Now, don't worry. You are healing nicely. The wound…"

I placed my hand on the spot. Nothing was there, not a shirt and not a bandage. There was no hole, no pain.

Mom reached for something on the end table. "The stone saved you," she said.

"We thought we were going to lose you," Dad offered, sitting on the other side of my bed, and reaching for me.

"What are you wearing?" I asked because Dad was quite suddenly what grandma would have called *a sight for sore eyes*. He still wore no shirt but had something like a blanket wrapped around him. His eyes were red, and his hair was tousled as if he'd been sleeping.

"Have you been crying?" I asked.

"Must be an airborne virus," Dad said, smiling.

I smiled back.

"After you are well…"

I couldn't believe Mom. Why couldn't I sit up? My stomach didn't hurt.

"The stone has put your body in a coma of sorts," Mom offered. "That you are awake means the healing is almost complete."

"What?"

"The death camas is stronger and more poisonous than anything else out there," Dad said. "Even the stone needs some time to work its magic."

I couldn't believe it, any of it. But then again, I could. I'd met Camas face to face and had come away wanting nothing to do with it.

"How much longer?" I asked.

Suddenly, the plane veered to the right and I slipped off the bed, clunking to the floor. Dad grabbed me and placed me back on the bed. "This has happened more times than I can count."

"How long have we been at war?" I asked.

"Practically since leaving Spore. Everyone is with us, whether in this space plane or on the dozens with us. But the cyborg breed is holding fast."

"They want the stone," I offered.

"And you," Mom finished.

"They just don't get it, even with me they will have no luck," I said.

"Even with torture?"

Chandra was suddenly in the room in human form. I wondered who was taking care of the spaceplane. She stumbled toward me, grasping the side of the bed to keep from falling. "How are you feeling?"

"I can't sit," I said.

She turned to my parents. "We need him – now," she said.

"Well. I can't help you NOW," I muttered under my breath.

"Just the same, we need you," Chandra sputtered, for I suddenly realized she was crying.

"I'm sorry," I said. "I really can't sit up."

She reached for the stone and placed it on my abdomen. "I want you to listen to me," she said, the plane shaking like an old man on crutches. "You are through the worst. The stone can help you with the rest."

I looked down at it sitting silently on my bare belly, and then just as suddenly realized that I was practically naked and Chandra was looking down at me.

I must have blushed because she said, not taking her eyes from my face, "That does not matter now. You will heal, and you will save us all."

There it was again. "How?" I asked.

"Close your eyes."

I did as I was told. If there was one thing I'd learned over and over, it was to listen, and after listening to follow through on what I was being told.

"Think of love," she said.

"Love?" I squeaked, feeling even more self-conscious now.

"The greatest love of all."

The greatest love I could think of was the love God offered, and there was no way I had that.

"The stone will help you," Chandra repeated.

"I thought of the love I had for my parents, for Neva and Stella. The love I had for God. And then, without me even knowing it, I thought of Chandra. Dear, sweet Chandra with the yellow hair.

Suddenly, as the plane rocked, and my parents held me on the bed so I wouldn't roll off, I felt the burning of the stone. It burned hotly, but it did not hurt, and moments later when I felt it was time to open my eyes, the burning sensation ceased.

I looked into the brilliant green eyes of the girl/monophylum I had grown to love and smiled.

Chandra looked on me and smiled back. "Stand!" she commanded.

I took the stone in my right hand and leaped off the bed.

"Great!" she offered, taking my hand. Together we ran to the 'room' as my parents more than likely stood still, their mouths gaping watching the scene. We gathered around the others. To be honest, the screen was a *sight for sore eyes*. There were many ships, all of them damaged to some extent, all of them fighting.

Bronty stepped away from the console.

"I must go," he said. "I am glad you are well."

Walking to the transport, he was gone in seconds.

What I'm going to tell you next might just be the most unbelievable thing you have ever heard, but I want you to hear it. Minutes that seemed like hours following Bronty's transport to one of the other planes to assist his comrades, I saw another face. It was as if they'd crisscrossed in the sky or something.

I was suddenly feeling the presence of the death camas at my back. A sickly feeling entered my soul even before I turned to face him head-on. It was like death was wrapping me around its gray fingers, taking away my very breath.

Hurling me beyond the console, Camas took the steering mechanism with his thin, black arms, and turned the plane away from our friends in space. We were suddenly traveling in the opposite direction, soaring through the skies away from the assistance we needed to survive.

I couldn't see my parents, but I could feel them. They were still alive. Damaged yes, fallen, yes, but still breathing. Chandra was speaking to me but I couldn't understand her words.

In the minutes since my last healing, I had thought of the iron pillar. This was the key. But I hadn't had the time I needed to reflect on the connection I was sure was there. And now I was on the floor and the death camas was steering the plane away.

"You thought to defy me, but we shall see what becomes of your plans. I have the cyborg Ursus on my side, and together, we will take over the planets!"

It was amazing, but during the time I knew the beast bears were making changes to their bodies so that they might live forever, I had never once found the place where the transformations were taking place.

"And you wouldn't have, either," smirked the death camas, funneling our plane through the black sky. "We take special precautions, precautions you would have to puncture to see."

"Like the cave of the green-eyed monster?" I asked.

"You are a smart one."

"But it's gone now."

"We had to move the initial place of transformation when the stupid humans lost their planet."

The thought of where the transformations had been taking place, gave me the creeps, but I tried not to show how I was feeling. I tried to think of death at that moment, hate, misery... but the thoughts wouldn't come. All I could think about was love. Love had entered my soul, and I was almost sure it would never leave me again.

"You cannot hide much from me," the death camas spit. "And I would advise you not to stand."

Blinking up at the blackened monophylum, I couldn't help but wonder why he'd become so blackened. Even my friends who had died had never looked so sickly.

"I am the great one, and it is only natural that I would have the color of what comes to me so naturally."

I swallowed.

"Do not worry. We will land soon, and I will take you and your loved ones away from here. You will die an honorable death."

Now I couldn't swallow. Tears glistened as I felt for the stone within my pocket. It burned my fingers. Looking up at the console, I could see we were no longer alone.

Curl, Presda's former guard, stood before me. I knew without even really knowing, that he was the new leader for the Ursus breed. Though he wasn't as large as Grude had been, he was definitely superior to the form of Presda, his previous master.

"We are almost there!" Curl shouted. He sauntered over to Camas and draped a hairy arm over the monophylum's shoulder.

"Remember what I told you," Camas offered.

The hairy arm was removed. "When will we kill them?" he asked.

"Soon. I want it to be a grand feast." The monophylum didn't look at me, his eyes riveted on the console. The stone burned between my fingers, but I held on. The time wasn't yet.

"You may use the stone in good time – to our benefit," Camas said. At that moment the rays of the red star penetrated the hull of the spaceplane. I closed my eyes for help. The iron pillar was distinctly in my mind. I tried to read the inscriptions, but they were foggy; I couldn't even see my name listed. Where was Chandra? Where were my parents?

As the space plane landed, I was pushed toward the opening. The air was a crisp burn when I stepped out, and the pillar just a few feet ahead.

"You may read the inscription if you wish," Camas muttered, walking in front of me, while Curl walked behind. "You may try your deceits of transportation, but you will not make it."

Camas grinned evilly back at me and I knew I wasn't the only one being led to their death. I could feel the breath of my mother and hoped my father was with her. I could feel Chandra, though I still hadn't seen her.

The hot sands brushed my legs as I reached the iron pillar and was allowed to touch its surface. It wasn't hot as I expected. The iron was cold to the touch, and there were only two inscriptions. The first spoke of Chandra as the Guardian, "Oh Chandra, Guardian of everlasting…" it read. And the second: "Bring ye the savior, Aaden to the temple of forever."

"What does it mean?" I asked.

The death camas laughed. "You tell *us.*"

The portal opened. "Inside," said Camas. I felt a push at my back from Curl and stumbled inside. Just as before, I was taken down a long and winding tunnel. It was still lit by some source I'd never been able to discover, although my thoughts had sometimes turned to the glass walls within the chambers. Perhaps they held a power that lit the tunnels.

Once inside the bare room – for this time there was no wooden table, no chairs, no food hanging from the ceilings, not even places to hold us – I finally turned to see my parents. They appeared to have aged before my very eyes, and Chandra, now in her monophyla form, reached for me. Her slim hand found my wrist.

"Now you see why you must help us," she said.

My mom blinked over at me, a small tear creasing her left eye. "This is the last time," she said. "Either we... or we die here like the others."

The word she'd not said was 'escape,' but I knew her thoughts, just as I'm sure the death camas and the Ursus, Curl, knew.

"What has happened to Bronty?" I thought to ask.

"You don't know?"

I searched my thoughts for an answer, and one came.

"He is still alive?"

"Many have died, but he is holding on, hoping for release."

"We must take action now," I said. "Curl!" I spoke within my mind. "I'm ready!"

The Test

In a blink, Curl was before me. I could smell him, hear him as he walked towards me and the others within the chamber.

"I have what you need," I said. "All the love I can give you is found within this stone."

I pulled it from my pocket and held it high. The stone glowed a brilliant green, casting even greater light against the lit walls. And then, in a rush, the green light penetrated the chamber. There was no end to it.

"Love is what you seek," I said. "I will help you to receive it."

The beast hovered above me. "What do I do?" he asked.

"Touch the stone."

"You think to trick me!"

"I will hold the stone; I will keep the love within it. Do not be afraid."

My mother gasped from behind me. I could feel Chandra's love, my father's strength. They were all in this with me. Though I wasn't sure at that moment if they understood what I was going to do, I felt their support. I wasn't alone in this. I was never alone in this.

"Touch the stone!" I repeated.

At that moment, the beast reached for my hand. As I felt the pressure of Curl's paw, Camas entered the room. "Stop!" it shouted. "The journey will be mine!"

Curl blinked, and removing his paw from my hand, turned and roared at his master. "I will touch the stone! I was given the power after Grude perished!"

"Your power is imagined! Wasn't it I who brought our species together! Wasn't it I who promised your master the takeover of planet Earth?"

"And how good was that promise?"

Camas spit. "You would not be here if it wasn't for me. Your struggle to live in the eternal realms forever would never have been satisfied!"

"What? You consider this slowly dying flesh to be eternal?"

I thought of the smell then, like decaying fruit, and I had my answer. Sure, the cyborg changes had granted the Ursus breed a greater lifespan with more physical power, but in the end, there would still be an end for them without the ultimate power of the green stone.

Curl turned to me, placing his hairy paw on my own. Camus jumped for us, and in just that instant, the walls of the prison shook. I clutched the stone, feeling for the first time the love God yet had for our adversaries

– the feeling was miraculous. As the rumblings continued, I knew that God could see them in the past, the present and the future.

"Now!" I screamed to the others in my head. During those few moments of jealousy between my two enemies, I had spoken to my parents, and to Chandra about what would happen next.

The stone burned within my hand and closing my eyes we traveled to Bronty's vessel. He suddenly stood before me like a grand warrior. As I'd predicted, he hadn't been captured. I didn't even need to look at the console to know what condition his plane was in. As the plane shook, Bronty placed his human hand on mine. Chandra, in human form, placed her hand on top of mine and my parents followed last. It took only a moment.

I knew where the temple was, but it was held in the past. As the plane rumbled, we held the stone close together – until the space plane stopped shaking and we'd been transported to the surface of Earth.

We slipped easily into the Green-Eyed Monster. Five ships followed us – more creatures from Spore and Sever that I hadn't yet been able to count.

The walls glistened in remembrance of the past. We sheltered the space planes under what I was soon to learn was a veil of forgetfulness. We left them inside the temple and retreated without the caves.

Only then did I look down.

My clothes were dirty, my shoes had somehow managed holes in both toes, and my hands looked as though they had come through a wind storm.

Of course, they had.

I didn't see my face but I knew how it must look. When I saw it later, in the coolness of the mountain lake, I could only smile at myself and wonder what I could possibly venture through next.

So, I was still 10 years old. My parents hadn't changed, and Chandra was still the girl with the yellow hair. But she seemed younger somehow.

"There's something I must tell you," she said, sitting close to me.

Earth was just as I remembered it before the grand explosion when Mercury had crashed into it, only this time it was not summer but spring. In the distance, I could see my parents embracing. I wondered what they were saying to each other. I wasn't even tempted to try and listen in. Through the transport of going back in time, all of my senses appeared to be sharpened. I could see colors deeper than before and hear things – even tiny bugs walking through the grass.

"What?" I asked.

Chandra blushed. In human form, she was truly beautiful.

"Neva and Stella. They healed your mother before their deaths. It was the last they could give."

I thought of my mother's hand after I'd awoken, healed from the poison of the death camas.

"I wondered," I said.

"They loved you so much," she said.

"I know. I loved them too."

"How did you figure it out, about the pillar, I mean?"

"It just seemed to fit. The pillar is the gate to the temple of forever."

Chandra smiled and placed her hand on mine. The stone was already in my pocket.

"How did you know that it would take all of us to transport us back through time?"

"That seemed to fit, too. Where the truth of the green stone was one of jealousy for Curl and the death camas, I knew the opposite would also be true."

I touched Chandra's hair. "You look much younger," I said.

"I am the same age as you," she answered.

"How?"

"Don't you know? I can transform…"

"Then, this is your true self?"

Chandra nodded.

"But I thought…"

Yes, I have lived for a millennium – perhaps longer, but this is my true age."

"I don't get it," I said.

She giggled now, and all I could think about was kissing her.

"Look at your parents. They seem happy."

I looked over at them again. They were still hugging each other.

"I have a question," I asked.

"You can kiss me later," she said.

I must have blushed then. "No… um… if you are really human, why did you get so angry when Stella lied? That shouldn't have mattered to you."

"Why not?"

I rolled my eyes. "Because, dummy, you are human. Humans lie all of the time."

"And you?"

I gulped. "I lie too. Isn't that pretty normal?"

"That depends on who you ask," she said, looking up at the sky. "I mean, when I decided to surround myself with the monophyla's ways, I also highly considered their spiritual truths. I guess you could say I took some of their ways as my own."

I didn't know what to say to that, but my mom came to mind. I couldn't help remembering once again how often she lived her own life with her old customs like washers and dryers and fixing meals with her bare hands instead of allowing the generator to do it. Perhaps Chandra was a little like that; taking on what she wanted in life though others might not understand why.

I looked over at her.

"You can kiss me now," she said.

I wanted to laugh. But then, not to miss the opportunity, I didn't ask any questions.

For a moment or two, it seemed as though I was traveling in space without a space place. At the very least, I was floating while still remaining planted on the ground. I didn't dare open my eyes, though I knew I would see into Chandra's green eyes if I'd been able to manage it.

When I opened my eyes, she was smiling at me.

"Have you seen Bronty?" I asked.

Chandra laughed. "Of course. He's gone to the lake."

"When?"

"Just after we landed. He can get there much quicker than he used to."

I thought of my dear friend, Bronty and all he meant to me. It wasn't fair that he had to be old, and we could no longer be friends in the same way. But at least he was alive.

"You are forgetting something," Chandra said, standing, and looking toward the lake as if she could see him, and maybe she could. "All of us are our true age."

"You mean, Bronty is young, my age?" I asked.

"Yes."

And then another thought entered my mind, dancing within its realms. "Neva. Neva is here?"

I waited for the answer. If Neva was alive, then maybe Stella.

"You're right on both counts," Chandra said into my mind.

"The others…" I began, but Chandra was ahead of me.

"All is the same as before. The wicked Grude is yet alive, along with Curl, Presda and the others."

"The death camas."

"Unfortunately, yes. The Earth and all of its inhabitants have not yet been destroyed. And now you have brought with you all of the children and the old ones. They will not have to die."

"But won't the evil ones come for us?"

Chandra was silent.

"Well?"

"I will always be grateful to Stella," Chandra offered.

"You're changing the subject," I said. I knew Stella to be a genuine creature of love, and a companion to Neva, but something else was beyond Chandra's eyes, something I was just beginning to make out.

"She lied," I said.

"Yes," Chandra answered. "She lied about taking a memory that she really didn't take. All to save you so that you could do what you have done."

"But surely, this little thing…"

Chandra's eyes misted over. They were still beautiful, though large pools filled her green eyes and fell down her cheeks.

"Monophyla do not lie, and she will yet have to take responsibility for it."

"We believe in forgiveness on this planet."

"I know."

Chandra looked away from me. Bronty was making his way back.

"There is something else you need to know," she said, holding my hand even tighter. "And I want you to listen." She stopped, breathed in once more, and turned her eyes to the sky. The tears continued to slide down her cheeks.

"I have always been a girl."

I took the words in. Actually, I couldn't speak. What did she mean, 'I have always been a girl?' What else could she have been other than a monophylum? And then I knew.

"You are a girl," I said. "You're not monophyla at all."

"Yesss," Chandra replied, hesitating on the 's' for effect. "It was the only way."

"A cover-up?"

"Of sorts."

"If you'd really been a monophylum, you would have really had a problem," I said, thinking of the lie that would have been hers if this was the case.

"Yes. Perhaps that's why I was so angry with Stella when I found out her secret. I was doing the same thing, just in reverse order."

A chill raced up my arms and back. "So, now, I guess it's the Earth I am to save," I asked.

"The Earth," Chandra answered, leaning her yellow head on my shoulder.

"How am I to do that?"

"And the wickedness that still prevails," said Chandra softly. "The good news is that you'll have me, your parents, Bronty, and Neva and Stella to help you."

"But, the entire Earth?"

"So, you must be the lovebirds," Bronty said suddenly, making me jump. He sat down beside us. "Maybe I should go somewhere else."

I laughed. "Bronty! It is you! Do you think if we go back to my house that the Legos will still be there?"

"And your mom's old washing machine?"

"What's wrong with my washing machine?"

I looked up. Mom and Dad hovered above us like two UFOs. "I happen to like that machine." They sat, but they weren't alone. I didn't see Neva or Stella, but it was like the wind was bringing them to me.

"Mom?" I asked.

"Yes, son?"

"I love you."

"We love you, too," Dad replied. A sudden movement from behind produced my old friend, Neva. He smiled a crooked smile, his green eye blinking over at me.

"Neva!" I cried, reaching for him.

In an instant, he was on my shoulder just as I remembered.

"Where's Ste--?"

"Stella won't be found for some days yet," Neva said, "if she's found at all."

"What?" I thought about the lie, the lie that for all intents and purposes hadn't even been spoken yet. If we were back in time, just months before the Earth's destruction, then the lie that Stella had told those in the silver suits hadn't even occurred yet.

"Monophyla are not time-bound," Chandra said now, looking me in the eyes. "The past, present, and future are one and now. All that has occurred in their lives yet is now.

Neva jumped from my shoulder and stared up at me. "Truth is everlasting," he said.

"So, where is she?" I asked.

Neva wiped a lone tear from his eye. "We are in this moment, but I don't see her," Neva said.

"It's a cruel trick," I answered.

"Not a trick," Neva answered. "All monophyla serve but one purpose. To speak truth and direction. Nothing more."

"But you love her!"

The words shook me, though I had spoken them.

"Yesss."

I turned to Chandra. "You are the Guardian. Do something!"

"You are the savior."

The words found a place in my mind and whirled within the chambers of my heart. I had managed to get us here, back in time, back before the Earth was destroyed – for what? To save the planet and to have all of my loved ones with me – but one?